How to Dork Your Diary

怪诞DORK diaries 少女日记 [特别版]

［美］蕾切尔·勒妮·拉塞尔（Rachel Renée Russell）/ 著

叶红婷 / 译

湖南文艺出版社
HUNAN LITERATURE AND ART PUBLISHING HOUSE

博集天卷
CS-BOOKY

图书在版编目（CIP）数据

怪诞少女日记. 4 /（美）拉塞尔（Russell, R. R.）著；叶红婷译.
—长沙：湖南文艺出版社，2016.1
书名原文：DORK DIARIES 4
ISBN 978-7-5404-7419-5

Ⅰ.①怪⋯ Ⅱ.①拉⋯ ②叶⋯ Ⅲ.①日记体小说—美国—现代 Ⅳ.①I712.45

中国版本图书馆CIP数据核字（2015）第316685号

著作权合同登记号：图字18-2015-159

DORK DIARIES Book 3 1/2: How to Dork Your Diary by Rachel Renée Russel
Copyright ©2011 by Rachel Renée Russell
Simplified Chinese translation copyright ©2015 by China South Booky Culture Media Co.,Ltd.
published by arrangement with Writers House, LLC through Bardon-Chinese Media Agency
ALL RIGHTS RESERVED

上架建议：畅销·文学

怪诞少女日记. 4

作　　者：［美］蕾切尔·勒妮·拉塞尔
译　　者：叶红婷
出 版 人：刘清华
责任编辑：薛　健　刘诗哲
监　　制：蔡明菲　潘　良
联合策划：博集天卷
　　　　　咪咕阅读
特约策划：李彩萍
特约编辑：李乐娟
营销编辑：桂　欣　李　群
版权支持：辛　艳
版式设计：李　洁
封面设计：利　锐
内文排版：八度出版服务机构
出版发行：湖南文艺出版社
　　　　　（长沙市雨花区东二环一段 508 号　邮编：410014）
网　　址：www.hnwy.net
印　　刷：三河市鑫金马印装有限公司
经　　销：新华书店
开　　本：880mm×1230mm　1/32
字　　数：246 千字
印　　张：6
版　　次：2016 年 1 月第 1 版
印　　次：2016 年 1 月第 1 次印刷
书　　号：ISBN 978-7-5404-7419-5
定　　价：29.80 元

质量监督电话：010-59096394
团购电话：010-59320018

谨以此书献给你，

我亲爱的读者朋友们！

用它记下你的白日梦、

你构想的剧情以及你的涂鸦。

始终记得

让你内在的怪诞范儿闪耀哦！

这本日记属于

我！

私人机密文件

嘿，朋友！不准偷看内容，否则……!!

怪诞少女日记
土肥圆逆袭白富美 ♥
DORK diaries

星期五，在家，上午6:05

哦，我的天哪！

我刚刚做了一个非常非常可怕的噩梦！

那是我整个人生中最糟的事！

我吓坏了，几乎都没法写这篇日记了。

↙我，吓坏了

我冷汗直流，心怦怦直跳，脑子也因为这样强烈的痛苦木掉了。

那感觉就像……呃……马上要爆炸!

为什么?!

我梦见我的日记本在学校丢了!

是的! 在学校丢了! 这是多么让人抓狂啊!

奇怪的是，这个事情就像真实发生的一样。因为我一觉醒来，记忆中所有的那些细节都涌入脑海中，让我觉得更混乱了。

我无法想象不写日记会怎么样! 就好像我上瘾了或什么的。

在梦中，我非常绝望，后来在布里安娜玩具箱的底部找到了她的一个旧涂鸦本，于是退而求其次开始在那上面写日记。

但让我抓狂的主要是有人会捡到我的日记本，并看到里面所有超级隐私、超级难为情、超级秘密的那些东西。

我和蜜糖公主在亲吻所有可爱的小独角兽

布里安娜 绘

啊啊啊啊啊啊啊！

这是我在尖叫。

为什么？

因为如果我在布里安娜的涂鸦本上写日记，那就只意味着一件事……

昨天我的日记本在学校丢了！

在家，上午6:12

我觉得我可能精神崩溃了或者什么的，因为我突然就开始大哭起来，而且根本停不下来。

用完一盒纸巾后，我的房间完全是一片狼藉。

但是当我抽泣着要穿过那7盒纸巾时，我看起来就像一块巨大的软麻布。

长着一对眼珠子的软麻布。

我很想就那样躺在那儿，盯着墙壁生闷气。最后，我决定，该让我

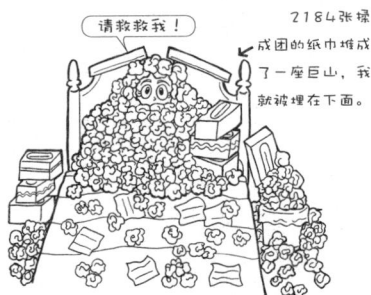

的屁屁从床上挪挪窝了。

为什么？

因为那些被我泪水浸透的纸巾，在我身边很快就开始变干变硬，很可能会把我变成一个"人形皮纳塔"①！

布里安娜就喜欢皮纳塔。

她做以下事情时我绝对会被吓到：

1. 把6盒橘色的嘀嗒糖一股脑地倒进我的喉咙。

2. 把我绑在电线杆上。

3. 用一个塑料球拍到处追着打我，直到我喷出或咳出一些糖果来。

那个孩子有很严重的问题。

我只是随口说说而已……

在家，上午6:30

我不能相信这件事真的发生在我的身上！

我记得最后一次看到我的日记本

---

① 皮纳塔（piñata），是一种用彩色纸做成的各种造型的容器，里面装有各种糖果或礼品，然后悬挂起来。过生日的小朋友蒙上眼睛用棍子打开皮纳塔，里面的礼品会散落出来，给小朋友惊喜！

是在昨天吃早餐的时候。

写完日记后，我就像平时一样，把它塞到我背包前面那个可爱的小拉链口袋里。

我要进行法语词汇测验，还有一个几何单元考试，所以在第7堂课之前我都没时间写日记。

当我打开背包前面的那个拉链口袋时，我的日记本就不见了！

成为整个学校里最怪诞的少女已经够糟的了，而现在每个人都会看到我的日记！

我是一个彻头彻尾的失败者，不，比那还要糟糕！

恶心的肉糜饼怪物

嗷呜嗷呜！

布里安娜 绘

好吧！这就是我吧？或者说这些画是在绝望地寻求帮助?!

布里安娜需要非常有效的抗精神

病药物治疗。越快越好！

我只是随口说说而已！

寻找丢失的日记本的计划

第1步：看看学校的失物招领处。（如果找不到，转到第2步。）

第2步：看看我上课的每个教室。（如果找不到，转到第3步。）

第3步：看看走廊、自助餐厅和图书馆。（如果还是找不到，转到第4步。）

第4步：钻进我的储物柜，"砰"地一声关上门，然后……死去！

这样彻头彻尾的惨败真是让我巨巨巨受伤，我几乎不能清醒地思考问题啦。

我敢说，我很可能得了某种非常

清洁工赫布发现724号储物柜散发出来的恶臭。

可怕又罕见的失调症，嗯……比如，压力过大引起的大脑——死机！

我的这个病让我几乎不可能继续写日记了。

到了这一步，我能做的唯一的事情就是，用布里安娜的涂鸦本，为我自己写下如何记日记的详细说明。

好消息就是，任何人都可以用我的这套小贴士写自己的日记！

学会如何让日记怪诞，对全人类来说都是既令人兴奋又有所获益的经历！

也许有一天，你的日记甚至还能救你一命呢，谁知道呢？

懂我的意思了吧？！

我是不是很有才呀？！

自我提示

你的日记可能会成为你最宝贵的财富。

所以，重要的一点是确定哪种类型的日记最符合你的个性。

怪诞日记小贴士#1

发现你的日记ID。

回答下面的问题，找出最适合你的日记类型。

1. 一个星期六的下午，你写完了所有的家庭作业，还有一小时的时间可以做你想做的任何事情。你决定：

A. 玩一局你最喜欢的刺激的电脑游戏或电子游戏。

B. 花点儿时间看看你的闺密（BFF①）一直赞不绝口的那本新书，放松一下。

C. 给朋友发发电子邮件或短信，或者上社交网站如Everloop与朋友保持联系。

D. 画你最喜爱的动漫人物，让你的创意之源绵延不绝。

---

① BFF是Best Friend Forever的缩写，永远的最好的朋友。

2. 你把日记本落在了上了三个小时的英语课上，然后你的暗恋对象在午餐时把它还给了你。那么你会：

A. 发给他一张可爱的电子动画答谢卡，并送给他最爱的糖块作为酬谢，给他一个惊喜。

B. 把肉糜饼塞进嘴里，然后冲进女洗手间，躲进一个小隔间，把自己锁在里面，在那里度过那一天剩下的时间。

C. 希望他读到你日记里关于喜欢他的那部分，这样他最后会叫你去参加学校的舞会。嘿，距离舞会只有一星期时间啦！

D. 当他赞美你为艺术展一直在忙活的那张自画像熠熠生辉、非常精美时，你满面羞红，并提出画一幅他的搞笑漫画像，表示对他的感谢。

3. 如果某件事情让你真的很烦心，你通常会：

A. 仔细思考这个问题一两小时，然后连吃三大杯本杰里（Ben & Jerry's）[1]的胖猴子（Chunky Monkey）冰激凌，弄成自我诱导的"脑冻结"，设法忘记那件烦心事。

B. 一整天私下里都在为这个问题而困扰，但当别人问起"你还好吗"，总是试着让每个人都相信你很好，而且没什么事情让你心烦，因为：

（1）你的问题对他们来说太复杂了，无法理解；

（2）要假装你自己很好，会让你筋疲力尽得不愿别人解释这件事。

C. 对愿意倾听你的任何人大声宣泄你的烦恼。因为如果你不开心，谁也别想开心！

D. 转移你自己的注意力，不要

———————————

[1] 美国冰激凌品牌BEN&JERRY'S是由两位童年玩伴BEN COHEN和JERRY GREENFIELD创办的，以口感香醇和口味新奇闻名。使BEN&JERRY'S快速驰名的原因，除了对产品品质的坚持外，还有该公司"社会公益向导"的企业使命。

担心。引导所有的负能量去做创造性的事情，比如，在你的储物柜里面画静物壁画，添置一个喷泉式饮水器、香薰蜡烛和瑜伽垫，在课间完全冷静放松下来。

4. 你的生日是在三个月前，你的奶奶为你织了一件暗黄绿色的毛衣，丑到不行，还比你的尺码大两个号，而且穿上比接触毒葛引起的严重皮疹还要痒，但你仍然需要给她寄去一封答谢信。你会：

A. 真诚地给她发一封快捷的电子邮件，告诉她你会永远珍惜她送的这份礼物，同时不经意地提到你是真的真的喜欢礼物卡，因为礼物卡只有一个尺码却适合所有人，而且通常不会引发皮疹。

B. 亲笔写一封真心诚意的答谢信，告诉奶奶她送的礼物你几乎天天都穿。但是不要说起你把它埋在后院，你老爸在给草坪浇水时偶然发现了，现在成了他打保龄球时的幸运衣这件事。

C. 加你的奶奶为线上好友，然后在她的网页上贴出你给她的答谢信，还要附上你自己穿着她织的那件毛衣的照片哦。这样一来，她的14个网友就能看见啦。不过，你还要戴上

你织的滑雪面罩，这样一来，虽然你穿着那件毛衣就像披着一身脏兮兮的牦牛皮，但你的1784位网友不会认出那就是你啦。

D. 画一张你自己穿着那件毛衣的画像，和真人一样大小，然后发给奶奶，表达你的感恩之心。因为多亏了她，当地动物收容所里的某个汪星人或喵星人非常幸运，将会在一件暖烘烘、毛茸茸、大两号的暗黄绿色的毛衣上生下她的幼崽。

5. 下面哪个选项最正确？

A. 你是一个非常精通技术的人。你具有团队精神，而且随时随刻准备迎接挑战。

B. 你待人友好，浪漫得无可救药。你喜欢蜷缩在舒服的毛毯里，做白日梦。

C. 你是个乐天派，有很多的朋友。你的生活中经常发生一些戏剧性的事件。

D. 你富有创造力，热爱艺术、

音乐、戏剧和诗歌。你拥有独特的个人风格，稍微有些急躁和犀利。

6. 你听到消息说你闺密的橄榄球队刚刚赢得了区域赛冠军。你会：

A. 给她发条短信："你赢啦，姐们儿！恭喜！"

B. 见到她的时候给她一个大大的拥抱表示祝贺。

C. 给她发一条你异常兴奋地大喊大叫的语音信息。

D. 亲手做一张海报，上面写着"你吊炸天"，贴在她的储物柜上面。

7. 你正打算洗你最爱的那条牛仔裤，发现后面的裤兜里竟然有10美元，那是你上次临时帮人看小孩挣来的。现在你是有钱人啦！你会怎样犒赏自己呢？

A. 买张票去看那部根据你最爱的小说改拍的大片。你一直在等它出来，好像等了一万年一样！

B. 去吃精美的纸杯蛋糕！啧啧啧啧啧！

C. 买唇彩！商场里有买二送一的大促销！

D. 给iPod下载音乐。最近你听了一些新曲子，还真是悦耳动听！

8. 你去参加睡衣派对（slumber party）①，现在到了游戏时间，你愿意玩下面哪个游戏？

A. 一起跳舞。

B. 游戏人生②。

C. 真心话大冒险。

D. 画图猜词。

现在，回头看看每个问题你选择的哪个答案。

ABCD你选的哪个最多？

我选的大部分是_____。

————————————

① 睡衣派对（slumber party），指一帮年轻的朋友穿着睡衣通宵畅谈的聚会。

② 游戏人生，是类似"大富翁"的一款棋盘类游戏，玩家可以在游戏中依靠转盘和自己的意愿走上各种不同的人生之路，模拟人生，拥有更多的不确定性，耐玩度因此大增。

大部分是A：

你很聪明，充满好奇，你喜欢学习新事物。你会非常喜欢在电脑上写日记，条分缕析地详细记录你有趣的冒险活动和新发现。

大部分是B：

你善良而敏感，而且喜欢帮助别人。你会非常喜欢在日记本上写日记或写日志。你的梦想和情感都很神圣。你的日记就像你的闺密，与它分享你的一切吧。

大部分是C：

你友好而外向，喜欢和人打交道。你会非常喜欢写博客。选择一个绝妙不凡的网络ID，和你的朋友们分享你激动人心、精彩纷呈的生活吧。

大部分是D：

欢迎来到我的
博客！
真诚的自白！
闲言碎语！
黑暗秘密！

你富有创造力又独立，你是一个有天赋的艺术家。你会非常喜欢在速写簿上记录你的思想。让你内心最深处的感受激发你创作抒情的诗歌、绝妙的艺术和令人喜不自禁的涂鸦作品吧。

现在提炼出针对你的个性建议的日记形式吧！如果你喜欢，那你就找到了符合你的日记形式！不过，如果那不是最合适你的，试试其他的，并挑选出你觉得最舒服的日记形式吧。

祝你好运！

在家，上午7:10

今天我已经有点儿害怕去学校了。

内心的一个我想就此放弃，然后

重新回到床上睡觉。但是，我迫切地需要找到我的日记本，所以，宅在家里肯定无法作为一种选择。

一想到我们学校的一些人会看我的日记，我就觉得浑身都不舒服。今天早晨我觉得非常恶心，几乎什么东西都没吃。

布里安娜给佩内洛普小姐做了一顿丰盛的美味早餐，对我也没什么帮助。

不好意思！但佩内洛普小姐只是一个笨笨的小手偶！就算是个白痴，只消看一眼就知道她绝对不会吃那么多食物！

但最要命的是，布里安娜捣鼓的那堆脏东西彻底把我恶心到了。

为什么，为什么，为什么我不是个独生女呀?!！

佩内洛普小姐说：

"真好吃!"

我，费了九牛二虎之力才做到没把嘴里的食物吐出来！

自我提示

写那些让你开心的事情总是很有趣。但是，你知道吗？写一个糟糕的经历或失望的事情，有时也会让你觉得那个情况好多了。如果有一天你过得真的很不愉快，记得用你的日记帮助你发泄，通过这种方式消解你的沮丧。

怪诞日记小贴士#2

好事、坏事和糗事都要写

好事

我，今天我荣获了学校艺术展的第一名！

写出发生在你身上最好的事。你当时是什么样的感受？

_____

_____

_____

_____

_____

_____

写出发生在你身上最糟糕的事。
你当时是什么样的感受?

画一幅画:
发生在我身上最好的事!

画一幅画:
发生在我身上最糟糕的事!

坏事

我，麦肯
齐和杰茜卡毁
了我崭新的派
对礼服!

糗事

被相机拍到我和我的妹妹在奎兹奇斯比萨店登台表演。

写出发生在你身上最出糗的事。你当时是什么样的感受?

_____

_____

_____

_____

_____

_____

_____

_____

_____

_____

画一幅画:

发生在我身上最出糗的两件事

自我提示

日记、日记天天要记,确保你每天都写日记。即使你把日记本弄丢了,也要坚持在备用笔记本或你妹妹那烦人的涂鸦本上写日记。

我和佩内洛普小姐！

吃冰激凌

布里安娜 绘

怪诞日记小贴士#3

一直写呀写。

惊奇吧！这是一个突击测试！抓起一支铅笔或钢笔，立即记流水账，写下你今天发生的事情！一直写下去，直到你看到"停"这个字。

我一到学校就跑到办公室。我甚至没有等两个闺密克洛艾和佐伊。

学校秘书皮尔逊老师正往教师信箱里分发信件。

"嗯……打扰一下，请问有没有人捡到一本丢失的书哇？"我火急火燎地问。

"早上好，尼基。事实上，昨天还真有个学生上交了一本书！他说是在自助餐厅附近的过道里捡到的。"

我简直不敢相信自己的运气！好开心哪，我长舒一口气，我当时恨不得上前拥抱她。

"我的天哪！有人捡到了还把它上交了？"我兴奋地尖叫起来，"我非常肯定，那本书就是我的！"

谢天谢地，这个噩梦终于要结束了。

当皮尔逊老师把那本书递给我的时候，我看了一眼，心就沉了下去。

那不是我的日记本！

我还需要一本几何书，就像我的脑袋还需要开窍一样。真见鬼！我就是不明白我已经学过的那本书上的数学问题。

"嗯……谢谢。但这不是我的

书。"我喃喃地说，把书还给了皮尔逊老师。

"哦，那去失物招领箱看一眼吧。有可能在那里呢。"她鼓励我说。

我闭上眼睛，祈祷它会在那里。

请让我的日记本在失物招领箱里吧！

请让我的日记本在失物招领箱里吧！

请让我的日记本在失物招领箱里吧！

然后，我叹了一口气，走到放在角落里的一个大硬纸箱面前。

我慢慢地打开箱子，仔细检查里面的每一件物品……

遗憾的是，日记本不在那里面。

我咬住嘴唇，眨了眨眼睛，强忍

我，在失物招领箱里各种稀奇
古怪的东西里寻找我的日记本

蜜糖公主
上等的午餐盒
灭蚤颈圈
宠物蜥蜴

失物招领

被咬过的
铅笔

牙套固定器

发霉的博洛
尼亚三明治

3D眼镜

缠在一起的
接发片

住眼泪。

"别担心，亲爱的。今天晚点儿它
肯定会出现的。"皮尔逊老师说，试图
让我心里好受些，"为了保证我们能找
到它，我会贴出一个告示，提醒我所
有的学生办公室助理们留意下属于尼
基·马克斯韦尔的一本书！好吗？"

那个时候，我的膝盖发软，我的
胃有作呕的感觉，我觉得我就要吐出
来了。

但这不是因为那块发霉的博洛尼
亚三明治。

也不是因为脏兮兮的牙套固定器。

也不是因为缠在一起的接发片
（虽然它的确以一种特殊的方式让人
觉得相当恶心）。

我突然意识到，我这个小小的日
记本的问题在出现转机前，很可能会

变得更加糟糕。

为什么？！

因为杰茜卡·亨特是学生办公室
的助理！

而杰茜卡的闺密是麦肯齐·霍利
斯特！

而每个人都知道麦肯齐·霍利斯
特对我恨之入骨！

就算我的日记本在某个时刻被交
到失物招领处，麦肯齐也非常有可能
截获，然后读我的日记，再然后把每
页的内容贴得学校到处都是。现在我
已经很惨了，她这么做就是为了让我
的生活比现在更惨！而对此我什么都
不能做。

除了直接冲到女洗手间，陷入巨
大的精神崩溃中……

啊啊啊啊啊啊！

（这是我在尖叫！第二次！）

自我提示

警告：

遗憾的是，父母、淘气的弟弟妹
妹、朋友、死对头，甚至是完全陌
生的人，都爱看不属于自己的日记。

千万，永远不要
把你的日记本放在
爱管闲事的小人
会偷看到的地方！

哦，我的天哪，
尼基！你在写日记
吗？我能看看吗？

哦，这个嘛。它只是一
本书，我从医生那里弄到
的，嗯……有臭脚丫子味。

如果有人看到你在写日记，你会
说些什么来应付他们呢？在下面写下
四种不同的回答：

嘿，那是你的日记本吗？！

千万别听信任何人对你说写日记
很傻，或者写日记很幼稚。实际上，
反思自己的感受、观点和经历是一个
非常成熟的行为。如果有人对你写日
记说什么粗鲁无礼的话，你会怎么回
应呢？

只有怪诞的人才有日记本！

你会怎么伪装你的日记本？在下
面的两页纸上画出假封面：

假封面#1

假封面#2

英语课，上午8:00

等赶到第一节课的时候，我已经完全上气不接下气了。

我疯了似的在我的课桌周围、台面上和书架上四处翻找。但都没有我的日记本的踪影！我当时心想："这下好了！"

我瘫坐在座位上，闭上眼睛，按摩我两边的太阳穴，努力地在脑海中回放昨天的事情。

如果我真的不知怎么弄丢了日记本，谁会在周围捡到它呢？我怀疑地仔细打量教室里每一个"潜在嫌疑人"。

就在这个时候，我想起来了，昨天是克洛艾和我一起走到教室的。和平时一样，她一路都在不停地絮叨她刚看完的那本最新的小说。书名叫……

"天哪，尼基！这是世界上最棒的书！我一读就根本停不下来！

"那个有才的画家痴迷于画一个超可爱的男孩，那是她在心里虚构出来的。后来，有一天，他成了一名新学生，出现在她的学校里。而且他能读懂她的心思！

"涂鸦小子看起来真是个善类，直到画家迷恋上了汉克·芬恩，那是在她美术课上出现的一个男孩，比涂鸦小子更可爱。他画了一张她的素描作为课堂作业，还和她分享了一个双层奶油巧克力纸杯蛋糕。

"当涂鸦小子开始表现出可怕的嫉妒时，那位画家断定，她别无选择，只能偷偷擦掉所有的画作摆脱他。

"后来，她完全崩溃了，因为涂鸦小子偷走了她所有的橡皮擦，这样一来她就没法擦掉他啦。然后他又开始吃纸，以获取超能力和不死之身。

"尼基，你也是个画家，我想你肯定会喜欢这本书的！"

我当时说："嗯……谢谢，克洛艾！我已经迫不及待地想看了！"

接着，她递给了我她的那本《夺命涂鸦小子》，我拉开背包拉链，把书塞了进去。

我的日记本很可能就是那个时候不小心掉出来的……

难不成是克洛艾捡到了？！

不得不承认，克洛艾无可救药地痴迷言情小说。

而且她什么都读。汤料罐上的标签、唇彩管上的说明……

如果她捡到我的日记本，还看了，而且很爱，很爱，很爱里面各种古怪的剧情怎么办？！

我知道这听起来可能真的很愚蠢！……但是，如果克洛艾真的把我那些非常私密又傻傻的悲情故事当成了畅销系列书，我该怎么办呢？！

再拍成一鸣惊人的好莱坞大片？！

甚至还不告诉我呢？！

那我很可能绝对、永远都打不开

这个结。我的人生也会完全被毁掉。

　　然后，许多年后，克洛艾和我碰巧在街上看到彼此……

　　亲爱的尼基，如果我没捡到你的日记本，我不会出名，也不会有这么有钱。请允许我往你那个小杯子里至少放一个25美分的硬币吧！

我 →
← 克洛艾

　　嘿，这都有可能发生！为什么我的生活如此无可救药、暗无天日?!

自我提示

写日记不仅仅是描述你是什么样的人，还在于发现你是什么样的人。

　　这就是深入挖掘并审视你的想法和感受很重要的原因。要非常自在地写你自己的事情！

　　怪诞日记小贴士#5

　　一切都围绕着我，我自己。

　　如果你能回答下面的每一个问题，你就上道了，将会写出极棒的日记！

什么事让你非常开心?

_____

_____

_____

_____

_____

_____

什么事让你非常伤心?

_____

_____

_____

_____

_____

_____

你生活中的最大成就是什么？

你最害怕的是什么？

你最骄傲的是什么？

你心目中最伟大的英雄是谁？

你最尴尬的事是什么？

你长大以后想成为什么样的人？

你最喜欢的三个电视节目是什么?

_____

_____

_____

_____

_____

_____

你最喜欢的三本书是什么?

_____

_____

_____

_____

_____

_____

你最喜欢的三部电影是什么?

_____

_____

_____

_____

_____

_____

你最喜欢的三首歌是什么?

_____

_____

_____

_____

_____

_____

你最喜欢的三个流行歌手是谁?

_____

_____

_____

_____

_____

你最喜欢的食物是什么?

_____

_____

_____

_____

_____

你最不喜欢的食物是什么？

你在无可救药地暗恋着谁？

在这个世界上，谁是你最好的朋友？

你想去哪里闲逛？

法语课，上午9:50

救命呀！今天变成了有史以来最糟糕的一天！

就在上法语课之前，为了我那失踪的日记本，我决定搜一搜所有女洗手间。

猜猜我碰到了谁？

提示：她正在照镜子，往嘴唇上涂第17层幻彩苹果味润唇膏。

你猜对了！

就是麦肯齐·霍利斯特！

注意到这一点：她竟然对我很友好！

当然，这让我觉得超级可疑。

尤其是她撞到了我，然后表现出一脸无辜和歉意的样子，就好像整个事情就是个意外一样。

"啊呀！我刚才撞到你了，尼基。但这完全是个意外！对不起！我希望你能接受我的道歉。顺便问一下，这个唇彩的颜色和我的鞋子搭吗？"

我简直不敢相信我的耳朵！麦肯齐竟然为她的笨手笨脚道歉，另一方面还在时尚方面问我的建议？这个丫头从哪儿学的这一套呀？汪星人会服从学校吗？我只是说说而已！

不知怎么的，一离开卫生间，我就注意到，走廊里的每个人都对我指指点点，嘲笑我。

而我一点儿都不知道这是为什么。

好吧，惊到了！我惊到了！

麦肯齐刚才了我一个小小的，嗯，"礼物"……

我，麦肯齐的小恶作剧让我当众丢脸

在法语课上再见到她的时候，我真想偷偷溜到女卫生间，借用一卷那里的卫生纸，但我不得不克制自己的这个想法。

为什么？

因为我内心阴暗而邪恶的那一面想在课堂上把那卷卫生纸塞在她的屁股后面。

我，让麦肯齐小尝一下自食其果的滋味！

邪恶的我

不管怎么说，当她大摇大摆走到我课桌边上时，我有点儿惊讶。

"据可靠消息来源说，你把你的小日记本弄丢啦。如果你所有的秘密都泄露出去了，那该多可怕呀。所以呢，我给你带来了一些重要消息！"

我惊讶得合不上嘴，我的心脏也狂跳不止。哦，我的天哪！麦肯齐知道我的日记本丢了？！

难道她已经从杰茜卡那里找到了我的日记本？我最糟糕的噩梦要变成现实了！

对于她说的消息，我有一种非常不好的感觉。

"说实话，麦肯齐，如果，你不插手我的私事，哪怕一次，对我来说那就是新闻了。"

这个时候，她用那双冰冷的蓝眼睛就那么盯着我。

她瞪了我一眼，昂起下巴，大摇大摆地回到她的座位上。

我会搜遍整个学校，直到找到你的日记本。等我做到了，你会后悔的！

我已经后悔了！后悔和你说话，你的口气闻起来就像你早晨吃了香肠煮豆子一样！

我讨厌麦肯齐大摇大摆的样子！

但现在我脑子里有两个让我心神不宁的问题：

1. 她会在我前面找到我的日记本吗？

2. 如果她做到了，她会用早已储备好的什么邪恶、残忍又歹毒的计划来对付我呢？！

麦肯齐恶魔般的眼神穿过教室注视着我，我很难集中精力上我的法语课。

我发誓！那个丫头到时候会非常后悔的！

我和蟑螂马克斯

去散步　　　布里安娜 绘

我刚刚是不是看到小蟑螂马克斯被皮带拴着的？！

好吧，我放弃！

关于这件事，毫无疑问的是……

我完蛋了！

自我提示

你永远都不会知道，你的日记会不会落到坏人手中。以防万一，要确保用一些只有你懂的代码！

怪诞日记小贴士#6

在必要的时候，进入秘密代码模式！

我和克洛艾、佐伊常常讨论CCP（辣妹）那伙人，在一起GGG-ing（咯咯咯地笑，吧啦吧啦地聊和打扮得闪闪亮）。将你和朋友们经常用的代码及其含义列出一份清单吧。

_____

_____

_____

_____

_____

_____

_____

_____

_____

_____

_____

你也可以赋予这些缩写新的含义，那么就没有人能破解你们的代码啦！

WCD＝韦斯特切斯特中学或世界级怪咖或：

_____

_____

_____

_____

_____

_____

_____

LOL＝放声大笑或可憎地大声笑或：

_____

_____

_____

_____

_____

_____

_____

_____

OMG=哦，我的天哪或:

_____

_____

_____

_____

_____

_____

BRB=马上回来，或忙着拯救蝙
蝠侠或:

_____

_____

_____

_____

_____

CCP=辣妹或:

_____

_____

_____

_____

_____

_____

BTW=顺便说一下或:

_____

_____

_____

_____

_____

_____

RCS =过山车综合征或:

_____

_____

_____

_____

_____

_____

TTYL=回头和你说或：

_____

_____

_____

_____

_____

_____

_____

JK=只是开个玩笑或：

_____

_____

_____

_____

_____

_____

_____

自我提示

你可以花很多时间在日记本里一笔一笔地写，也可以通过艺术作品表达自己。

试着添加图画、涂鸦、卡通画和连环漫画。它们可以很严肃、很艺术、很情绪的、也可以就那样简简单单、傻傻的。如果你是一个超级有天分的艺术家，那就创作一幅杰作；或者尝试画一些简笔人物画；或者像你以前在幼儿园那样，描出手的轮廓，然后把它变成火鸡。尽情享受这种乐趣吧！

怪诞日记小贴士#7

释放你心中的艺术家！

下面是一个四格漫画，叫作"我的日记剧本"（"格"就是里面艺术作品的方框的别称。）

?!

啊！

老师→

我以后不在课上写日记了。
我以后不在课上写日记了。
我以后不在课上写日记了。
我以后不在课上写日记了。

唉！ 我写
我写
我写
我写

现在，你可以创作你自己的四格漫画啦！但是在你开始之前，规划一下你要画的是些什么。

我的四格漫画名叫：

_____

_____

第1格：

第1格将包含一幅画：

_____

_____

_____

_____

里面的人物在说：

_____

_____

_____

_____

_____

_____

第2格：

第2格将包含一幅画：

_____

_____

_____

_____

里面的人物在说：

_____

_____

_____

_____

_____

_____

第4格：

第4格将包含一幅画：

_____

_____

_____

_____

第3格：

第3格将包含一幅画：

_____

_____

_____

_____

_____

里面的人物在说：

_____

_____

里面的人物在说：

_____

_____

里面的人物在说：

_____

_____

_____

现在，你可以在提供的空白处画你自己的四格漫画。玩得开心哟！

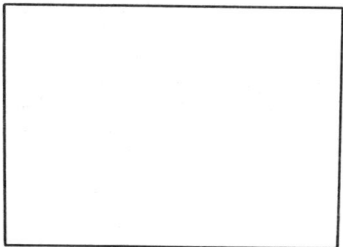

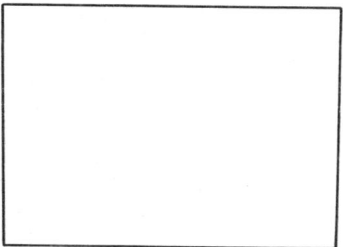

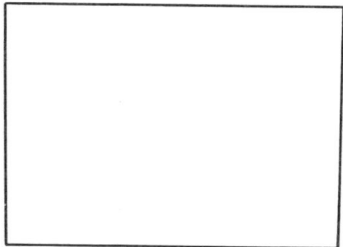

社会研究课，上午10:47

我开始觉得我的处境毫无希望了！

我查看了所有的走廊、图书馆和自助餐厅。刚才我又四处搜寻了社会研究课的教室。

但是仍然没有我的日记本的踪迹！

就在这个时候，我开始想会不会有人偶然捡到了它。

除了克洛艾，我昨天和谁接触得比较密切来着？

对了，可真是没脑子呀！答案就是——佐伊！！

作为图书馆的上架助理，克洛艾、佐伊和我在自习课期间要去图书馆。我们要把图书馆所有的书收集在一起，然后把它们重新摆放到适当的书架上。

不得不承认，我连昨天到图书馆有没有带我的日记本都记不清了。但是如果我确实带了该怎么办呢？！

哦，我的天哪！如果佐伊在收集那一大摞书的时候，不小心把我的日记本也收走了，该怎么办呢？！

如果她在把那些书放回书架时发现了我的日记本，并看了我的日记，

← 佐伊不小心把我的日记本收走了!

访谈录
我
佐伊·富兰克林
啊!

欢迎回来!今天的访谈嘉宾是尼基,来和我们分享更多她令人惊讶的悲催生活!

那该怎么办呢?!她将会有足够多的剧情,推出她自己的电视脱口秀……

现在,我已经完全泄气了,我想大哭一场。

但我还是把这种非常不舒服的感觉压在内心深处,我感觉很可能再也不会看到我的日记本了。

我无法相信这件事情就发生在我身上!

自我提示

日记本是你勾画未来人生目标的好地方。制订一些你在一个月或更短的时间内能够实现的短期目标。再制订一些长期目标,你可能要花费一年或更长的时间才能实现。

记住:跟踪你已经实现的那些目标,并设定令人兴奋的新目标。

怪诞日记小贴士#8

敢于梦想你的未来!

列出你想实现的3件事情:

明天:＿＿＿＿＿＿＿＿＿＿

＿＿＿＿＿＿＿＿＿＿＿＿＿＿＿＿

＿＿＿＿＿＿＿＿＿＿＿＿＿＿＿＿

＿＿＿＿＿＿＿＿＿＿＿＿＿＿＿＿

＿＿＿＿＿＿＿＿＿＿＿＿＿＿＿＿

＿＿＿＿＿＿＿＿＿＿＿＿＿＿＿＿

下星期:＿＿＿＿＿＿＿＿＿

＿＿＿＿＿＿＿＿＿＿＿＿＿＿＿＿

体育课，上午11:45

当克洛艾和佐伊两人跑过来的时候，我差点儿摔到体育馆的地板上。

"嗨，尼基！"克洛艾叫道，看起来有点担心，"我们今天早上在你的储物柜旁边等你，第2节课后又等你。我们都开始认为你可能是在家生病了或怎么的了。"

"是呀，现在见到你我们很高兴。"佐伊说，"不过，说实话，你今天看起来的确很低落。你没事吧？"她问道，给了我一个大大的拥抱。

我不配拥有像克洛艾和佐伊这样的朋友！

我曾怀疑我的闺密捡到我的日记本，读里面的日记，然后还让全世界都知道，为什么我会这样？我本应该一辈子都信任她们的！

一股内疚感向我袭来。这个时候，我决定告诉克洛艾和佐伊发生了什么事情。

我压低声音，近乎咬耳朵窃窃私语。

我简直不能相信，克洛艾和佐伊竟然在体育课全体同学的面前那样大声喊了出来！

每个人都听到了，并开始盯着我

实际上，我是有点儿低落，我想我，
呃，丢了……我的……日记，日记本！

?!!   ?!!

你丢了日记本？！

们看。

"嘘嘘嘘嘘嘘嘘嘘！"

我压低声音喊道："我正想着要
保密呢！顺便说一句，我提到麦肯齐
知道我日记本丢了的事吗？她也在找
我的日记本呢。"

"糟糕！"克洛艾说，她的脸皱
在一起，好像闻到了什么非常难闻的
气味一样。

"好了，小伙伴们，我想，那仅
仅意味着我们得在麦肯齐之前找到
它！"佐伊说，她的两只手放在屁
股上。

"对呀！麦肯齐还有她的那些辣妹
都敌不过我们三个！对吧？"克洛艾
说着，像跳爵士舞一样对我晃动双手。

我的心里百感交集，在开合跳进
行到一半的时候我就开始哽咽了。

如果我的日记本落在了这个学校
的任何地方，我的两个闺密——克洛

艾和佐伊肯定是能帮我找到的人。

或许事情根本就不是那样毫无
希望。

自我提示

你的日记本
是个好地方，可以
提醒你自己事情不
是总像你想的那么糟
糕。你可以用日记来安排一些激动人
心的事情和有趣的活动。感觉心情低
落？那就举办一个派对，并邀请你所
有的朋友，让自己高兴起来吧！

怪诞日记小贴士#9

不要成为派对上煞风景的人！玩
得开心，好好庆祝！

完成下面的练习：

这是我的派对！！

惊喜！你要为自己举办一个真正
的大派对，因为你值得拥有。

它将是哪种类型的派对？

□化装派对　　□睡衣派对

□泳池派对　　□舞蹈派对

□寻宝游戏　　□＿＿＿＿＿
　　　　　　　　（填空）

派对将在哪里举行？

_____

_____

_____

_____

_____

_____

_____

要提供什么食物？

_____

_____

_____

_____

_____

_____

我的派对客人名单

朋友

（列出一份你打算邀请来参加派

对的10个朋友的名单。）

_____

_____

_____

_____

_____

_____

特别嘉宾

（列出一份你打算邀请来参加派对的10个人的名单，他们可以是现在活着的，也可以是已故的，也可以是历史上的人物，也可以是你最喜欢的书籍、电影或电视节目中的角色，或是名人、职业运动员等。）

_____

_____

_____

_____

_____

_____

_____

_____

_____

_____

自助餐厅，中午12:25

午餐时，我无精打采，像行尸走肉一样。那道变味的砂锅菜散发的馊味甚至都没惹我心烦。

"我的日记本好像蒸发了一样，"我喃喃自语，"我不知道到底是怎么把它弄丢了。我怎么能这么笨呢？"

佐伊同情地捏了下我的肩膀："尼基，别自责啦。再说了，三个臭皮匠顶个诸葛亮！我们都好好回想一下，昨天吃午餐的时候你有没有带着日记本。我们就从昨天坐下来吃饭的时候开始。"

"嗯……"克洛艾挠了挠头，转了转眼睛，咂了咂舌。只有在真正陷入沉思的时候，她才会做出这样的举动。我几乎能听到她转动大脑时发出的"嘎吱嘎吱"的声音。"昨天午餐的时候？"

"嗯，佐伊打开了她的苹果汁，

抿了一小口。然后我说，'尼基，你是不是要吃那个炸薯条哇？'尼基说，'我本来打算吃的，直到你拿起它，闻了闻，又问我是不是要吃，我就不想吃了。'然后我又说，'这得谢谢炸薯条！'然后我问佐伊能不能尝一口她妈妈做的有名的蓝莓松饼，因为那些东西超好吃。接着佐伊说……"

"嗯，克洛艾，我们跳过所有琐碎的细节怎么样？"我尽最大的努力保持冷静地说道。

"好吧，老实说哦，我记不清昨天吃午餐的时候你到底带没带你的日记本。"克洛艾承认说，"但我的确记得你有一次倒盘子时不小心把它扔进了垃圾桶里。"

佐伊的眼睛亮了起来："哇哦！克洛艾说到了点子上。如果这样的事情发生过一次，那就会再次发生。尼基，或许……你把它给扔了！"

"哦，我的天哪！你俩认为我把日记本扔了？如果我真的扔了该怎么办呢？"我呢喃着说。

这时，我从餐桌边上跳了起来。

"快点儿，小伙伴们，13分钟后午餐就要结束啦！"

"我们要去哪里呀？"克洛艾

我，吃午餐时不小心扔掉了

我的日记本？！

问道。

"去垃圾桶那儿！"我扭头大声喊道。

"你一定是在和我开玩笑吧！"佐伊脸上露出恶心的表情。

"好消息是麦肯齐永远都不会想到去那里看看！"我再次觉得充满了希望。

我和克洛艾一路小跑着穿过自助餐厅，朝通向外面的后门走去，佐伊落在了后面。

"在我看来，我觉得麦肯齐并不是那么迫切地想看你的日记。"佐伊咕哝道。

当我们靠近垃圾桶的时候，过了三天的鱼条和变质的牛奶散发出的恶臭差点儿把我熏翻。

但是我不顾一切。

于是我咬紧牙关，屏住呼吸，然后细心地眯着眼睛往里看。

"我在一个快乐的地方！一个快乐的地方！一个快乐的地方！"佐伊一边往里面爬一边反复唱着。

她在做一个愚笨的冥想练习，但这一点儿都不起作用。

"你们知道，这个垃圾堆爬满了携带疾病的细菌，对吧？"佐伊唠唠叨叨地说，"等我一回到家，就把这身衣服脱下来，然后烧掉！"

克洛艾已经爬进去了，忙碌地掏着里面的垃圾。

但是你想知道真正奇怪的部分吗？

她看起来竟然非常享受这件事！

"如果我的日记本在这里的话，

克洛艾、佐伊和我在垃圾桶里搜寻我的日记本。

它很可能在最上面。"我说，一边猛拍一只过于友好的苍蝇。

遗憾的是，我在那些腐烂的食物中能找到的净是体育课上折断的曲棍球球棒和瘪篮球，还有上面判有"不及格"硕大红色字样的考试卷。它们当中没有一个是我的，我发誓！

"嘿！来看看！"克洛艾欢快地叫起来。

"哦，我的天哪！你找到了我的日记本？"我兴奋地问道。

"还没呢，但这顶柔软的帽子不是非常可爱吗？"她戴上那顶帽子，然后摆出一个造型，"现在我看起来像个明星啦！"

"它是好看，可我们得继续找。"我气鼓鼓地说。

一分钟后，我听到一声高分贝的

惊呼，"呀——"又是克洛艾！

"是什么？！是什么？！"我急切地问。

"哦，我的天哪！这可是最新一期的《吸血鬼帅哥》月刊哪！"

她把那本杂志搂在胸前，抱住不放。

"怎么会有人把这个也扔掉？谁捡到归谁！"

"行啦，克洛艾！"佐伊翻了翻白眼说道，"认真点儿！"

"切！我在找，一直在找哇！"克洛艾把一个垃圾袋放到旁边，然后弯下腰挑拣什么东西。

"哦——我的——上帝呀！"她尖叫起来。

我叹了口气。"这次，请告诉我是我的日记本。"

"是一只哈利抱熊啦！"她给了那只脏兮兮的泰迪熊一个紧紧的拥抱，"我要留着它。"

"这下好了！"我嘟囔道，一边看着我的手表，上面覆盖着厚厚的一层芥末，"午餐就要结束了，而我们才勉强扒拉了这里的表面。我不知道还能不能找到我的日记本。"

我从垃圾桶里爬了出来。

备受打击。这里真的真的太臭了。

"嘿！我知道什么可以让你开心起来，"克洛艾用一种非常烦人的尖声尖气的娃娃音轻轻地说，"来一个大大的拥抱怎么样！"

然后她将那只脏兮兮的哈利熊推到我面前。

我当时在心里说："哦！不！她不会的！"

咯咯咯咯！
咯咯咯咯！

克洛艾一定是彻底疯了。

而佐伊则事不关己高高挂起，咯咯咯地笑起来，像一只异常兴奋的花栗鼠。

但因为她们是我的闺密，我决定不对整件事心存芥蒂。

于是……我就抱了抱那只笨熊。

实际上我不好意思承认，那只哈利抱熊确实让我感觉好了一点儿。突然我就克服了那里的臭味！

自我提示

有时候，非常微不足道的东西也会引发最美好的回忆。把你去听那场精彩的现场音乐会的门票，或去看那部卖座大片的电影票都保存好；把你的闺密在数学课上传来的搞笑的小字条也保留好；把你在午餐纸巾背面画的暗恋对象的可爱涂鸦也收藏起来。你可以好好利用你的日记本，将它作为你喜爱的那些小物件的珍藏之地。

怪诞日记小贴士#10
珍藏你要丢弃的物品
找出会带给你美好回忆的两件物品。
把第一件物品粘贴在下面的空白处。

现在，记录一下你粘贴在上一页中的是什么，你是怎么得到它的，这样你就永远不会忘记啦。

_____

_____

_____

_____

_____

_____

现在，在这里粘贴第二件物品，并在下面做好记录。

_____

_____

_____

_____

_____

_____

_____

生物课，下午1:30

今天成了有史以来我在学校里最漫长的一天。

拜托，拜托，拜托让这一天快点儿结束吧。

我不知道我还能忍受多久。

到我去上生物课的时候，似乎整个学校都在八卦我那本丢失的日记本！我认真考虑了，要不就假装头疼，早点儿回家。

我尽最大努力不去理会教室里盯着我的所有目光和窃窃私语。但是对麦肯齐，我真的很难做到这样，她坐在教室的那一头，当着我的面就叽叽歪歪说我的闲话。

我当时正处于暴躁的情绪中，勉强对我的暗恋布兰登了一声"嗨"。尽管他给了我一个灿烂的微笑，并告诉我下课后有个重要的东西给我。

对不起，我那时最不想要的就是再上一堂额外学分课。尽管这通常意味着我和他会在实验室里一起多学习1小时。

我们学校有非常严格的规定，上课不许带手机，但是当麦肯齐坐在那里忘乎所以地发短信时，我看得惊呆了（还有一点点羡慕嫉妒恨）。我们

的金凯德老师当时在黑板上画分子图，然后唠唠叨叨地讲述那一天极其没劲的微生物课。

麦肯齐能够逍遥法外，为所欲为！这件事让人觉得非常悲哀，但却是真的。每个人都熟视无睹，甚至连老师们似乎也视而不见。

或者说我是这样认为的。

"二磷酸腺苷是由三磷酸腺苷断裂一个磷酸基而形成的分子，它会释放能量，被用于生物反应……麦肯齐·霍利斯特同学，我站在这里在全班同学面前打算讲课的时候，你似乎在忙着捣鼓你的手机呀！希望我没有打扰到你！"

我不相信我们的老师竟然会那样说！

全班变得非常安静，连一根针掉到地上的声音都能听见。班上的每个人，包括老师，都盯着麦肯齐。

但是那位小伙伴是那么忙于发短信，甚至都没有注意到这一切。

金凯德老师气急败坏，提高了嗓门："霍利斯特同学，能不能请你放下你的手机！现在立刻马上！"

很显然，麦肯齐一个字都没有听到。

金凯德老师被惹怒了，她走过去，就站到霍利斯特旁边。

但是麦肯齐还是全神贯注地继续发短信。

就在那个时候……

哦，我的天哪！太搞笑了！

麦肯齐几乎从座位上跳了起来。

金凯德老师真的没收了她的手机。

霍利斯特同学！

整个班哄堂大笑起来，有那么一瞬间我为麦肯齐感到有一点儿难过。

但那完全是她自己招来的！

"麦肯齐，规定你是知道的。我们对于在课堂上使用手机是零容忍。在我收到关于为什么不允许在课堂上使用手机的5页纸检讨后，10天之内我会把它还给你。你明白了吗？"

麦肯齐看起来糗死了。"我想——我想我明白了！"她结结巴巴地说。

"鉴于你的短信如此重要，以至于你打断了我们上课的时间，我想，你和我们大家都分享一下是最合适不过了。"

麦肯齐的脸色看起来绝对是铁青的。

金凯德老师眯着眼看了一下手机，然后大声念出了最后一条短信。

"布雷迪·格雷森发送：不行，那样太冒险了。我今天有早期橄榄球训练，但是我可以在那之后把它还给你。下午3点在体育馆见吧。"

全班人都在大声地笑。

让麦肯齐受够了窘迫之后，老师才继续讲课。

"对了，我刚才讲到哪儿了？……哦，二磷酸腺苷，我觉得是。二磷酸腺苷是由三磷酸腺苷断裂一个磷酸基而形成的分子……"

上完课之后，我无心逗留。

"嘿，等等！我想给你一样东西！"布兰登说着，一边伸手去拿他的书包。

"其实，现在我应该去找克洛艾和佐伊她们……"

"只耽误你一小会儿。我听说你的日记本丢了。所以，在你找到之前，我想把这个给你……"

布兰登递给我一个薄薄的用信纸包得四四方方的东西。

我打开，超惊讶地发现那是一个螺旋笔记本。

"这没什么特别的。只是我的储物柜里有两个多余的笔记本。我猜你能把它派上好用场。"

我就那样注视着他，一时说不出话来。

这是最近这段时间我收到的最甜蜜的礼物之一。

"谢……谢谢，布兰登！"我结结巴巴地说，脸疯了似的直发红，"它真是一个漂亮的……颜色！一共256页，花了3.97美元。我的意思是说……哇哦！"

他笑了，也脸红了："你喜欢它，我很开心。"

"是的，我喜欢。非常喜欢！"

"嗯，我想，明天我还会见到你的。"

"是的，还是在这儿！"

"拜！"

"拜！再次谢谢！"

我把那个笔记本放在我的背包里，然后走出教室。

但是在脑海里，我一直跳着我的史努比"快乐舞蹈"。

在那之后，我就像受到了过山车综合征的袭击一样。哦，我的天哪！

我觉得心里就像有1000只蝴蝶扑扇着翅膀飞来飞去。嘻嘻嘻嘻嘻嘻嘻嘻嘻嘻！

自我提示

有时候，你是不是想把一些事大声说出来，说出你的心声，但是你又有点紧张或害怕？

虽然你不想表现得粗鲁无礼，但告诉人们你到底是怎么想的、你有什么样的感受也会有好处。要不然，最后你只能在心里说说，这样除了你别人就听不到了。而过一段时间后，那多少会变得事过境迁了。

怪诞日记小贴士#11

把你只在心里说的所有事情全都写下来。

我大声说出来的是……

给你10美元帮我洗车怎么样？

嗯……那好吧

←爸爸

我→

我在心里想说的是……

有些什么事情是你只在心里说说，但又考虑说给别人听的?

1. 说给你的闺密

_____

_____

_____

_____

_____

2. 说给学校里并不总是对你超级友好的某个人

_____

_____

_____

_____

3. 说给你的父母

_____

_____

_____

_____

_____

_____

_____

4. 说给你的兄弟姐妹

_____

_____

_____

_____

_____

_____

5. 说给你的暗恋对象

_____
_____
_____
_____
_____
_____
_____
_____

几何课，下午2:00

啊啊啊！

那是我在尖叫！

我简直不能相信，刚才我把自己弄得像个彻头彻尾的傻瓜！！

克洛艾、佐伊和我决定课间再去查看一下失物招领箱。

主要是因为杰茜卡现在是第6节课的办公室助理，所以我们想在她之前找到日记本。

当我们走进去的时候，看到两个女孩坐在柜台后面的地板上，疯狂地把一些物品扔回到失物招领箱子里面。

发现她们是麦肯齐和杰茜卡，我们一点儿都不惊讶。

呕！ 真恶心！

失物招领

看到我们站在那儿，她俩似乎都感到有点震惊。

麦肯齐飞快地一把抓过她的包包，并拉上拉链："杰茜（Jess，杰茜卡的昵称），谢谢你帮我找到……我的……嗯，唇膏。上课见啦。"

杰茜卡走到柜台那里，冲我们露出她那非常灿烂的虚伪的笑容："嗨，你们好哇！有什么需要我帮忙的吗？"

要我和她谈论我的私事，没门儿！"皮尔逊老师在吗？"

"事实上，她不在。她去开会了，大约10分钟后会回来。有什么我能帮助你们的吗？"她说，一边瞟了一眼麦肯齐，同时还努力忍着偷偷笑。

"我希望你没丢什么非常重要的东西呀，"麦肯齐咆哮着说，"你知道的，比如封面上有个口袋的日记本之类的啦。不要浪费时间来找失物招领箱了，因为它肯定不在这儿！对吧，杰茜卡？"

克洛艾、佐伊和我简直不敢相信，她竟然当着我们的面就这么说。

现在，毫无疑问，我心里想的果然没错，麦肯齐已经找到了我的日记本。我肯定，她很可能就把它塞在她的包包里。

"麦肯齐，把我的日记本还给我。"我说道，直盯着她那对明亮的小眼睛。

"对！把它交出来！"克洛艾气鼓鼓地说。

"现在立刻马上！"佐伊也低声吼道。

麦肯齐只是撩了撩头发，然后瞪着我们。

我一点儿都不知道你们这群丢三落四的人在说些什么。我看现在你们该吃药了吧。

但是我有种直觉，她在撒谎。

"那不是你的，所以把它还给我！"我强烈地要求说。

"好吧，它可能在我这儿，也可能不在我这儿。你永远都不……"

麦肯齐话说了一半就停下了，好像被我们身后的什么东西打断了。她刚刚还紧缩的眉头迅速化成了灿烂却非常虚伪的笑容。

我转过身，温斯顿校长就在那个时候跨步走进了办公室。"下午好，姑娘们。"他说道。

"哦，我的天哪！看看这时间。得走啦。几何课见，尼基。"麦肯齐一把抓起她的包包，然后紧张地朝门冲去。

我与克洛艾和佐伊交换了一下眼神。她们便飞快地移步走到她的面前，堵住她的去路，这样一来她就不能离开了。

麦肯齐嫌恶地看着她俩，但为时已晚。

我深吸一口气："嗨，温斯顿校长。不知道您能不能帮我们一个忙，处理一个小问题呢？"

他停下来，调整了一下眼镜："当然可以！现在说说吧，什么事情有麻烦呢？"

麦肯齐无辜地眨巴着眼睛，试图掌控当时的局面："温斯顿校长，事实上，问题是尼基到这儿来似乎认为我拿了属于她的一本书。"

我突然打断了她说："我没有这么认为。我知道事实就是这样。"

麦肯齐吸了吸鼻子，装作一副快要哭起来的样子："我刚刚告诉她，我没拿她的破日记本。但是她不相信我。我不知道她为什么要对我说这些刻薄的话，亏我一直以来对她那么好，还给她提供各种免费的时尚建议。温斯顿校长，您就看看她吧。她真的需要时尚建议。我们学校的吉祥物蜥蜴拉里都比她的行头好得多……"

"那你怎么知道我的日记本丢了？还有它的封面上有个口袋？"我质问道。

办公室里的每个人，包括温斯顿校长，就那样盯着她，等着她做出回答。

麦肯齐咬着嘴唇，开始窘迫地扭来扭去。

"那个，其实……嗯，全校都知道呀。克洛艾和佐伊在上体育课的时候大声说出来的。还有你每天都在那上面写日记。就是这样我知道你的日记本封面上有个口袋。但是我发誓，它真的不在我这儿！"

"这种辩解可不会轻易作数，"温斯顿校长叉着手臂严厉地说，"我希望你们几个姑娘能把这件事情弄清楚，因为如果我介入的话……"

麦肯齐脸刷的一下红了，接着她瞟了一眼她的包包。

"好吧，尼基！如果你不相信我，那就请便！搜我的包包好了！"然后她就开始吸鼻子，眨巴眨巴眼睛控制更加虚伪的眼泪，营造出戏剧般的效果。

她从包包里掏出四支润唇膏、一些嘀嗒糖，还有一个刷子，把它们放在柜台上。

然后闭上双眼，交出她的包包，像是把她新得的小狗狗交出来，给一个残忍得超乎寻常的打狗队一样。

麦肯齐的包包是空的！

我完全惊呆了，所能做的就是盯着看。

这个丫头到底把我的日记本怎么着了？

"谢谢你，霍利斯特同学！"温斯顿校长赞许地说，"我非常满意你的诚实。"

但我完全困惑了！她怎么能那样玩我呢？

"那么……？！"温斯顿校长注视着我，手指开始不耐烦地敲着桌子。

"呃，我猜她……她根本没有拿我的日……日记本。"我低声喃喃地说。

我觉得尴尬极了。我真想一把抓过办公室的垃圾桶，把它戴在我的头上，遮住刚刚贴在我额头上的"白痴"两个字。

克洛艾、佐伊和我交换了一下不安的眼神。

"好了，马克斯韦尔同学，我觉得你欠霍利斯特同学一个道歉。"温斯顿校长说，这个时候麦肯齐笑得像一个刚刚得到翅膀的小天使一样。

我生气极了，真想……呸！一口唾沫吐过去。

我耗尽所有的意志力才忍住没有扇过去一巴掌，扇掉她那一脸得意扬扬、幸灾乐祸的笑容！

我低头凝视着我的脚，如鲠在喉，但努力地把这口恶气咽下去。

"嗯，对……对不起。"我嘟囔着说。

"啊？她刚才说什么？我听不见她说的。"麦肯齐像个娇生惯养、顽劣不堪的孩子一样抱怨道。

"我说'对不起'！"

"好了，马克斯韦尔同学，我希望，你下次再像这样错误地指控别人之前要三思而行。你明白了吗，小姑娘？"

我垂下头："是，校长……"

温斯顿校长瞟了一眼手表："好了，姑娘们，两分钟后我有个电话会议。很高兴我们能解决这个问题，让每个人都满意。"

然后他大步走进了他的办公室，关上了门。

克洛艾和佐伊陪我走回到我的储物柜那里，我的脑袋像在不停地旋转。我嘟囔道："我觉得自己真笨！对不起，我把你们两个也拖进这件事来了。"

"嘿，别为那个心烦了，"佐伊说，"我们也认为你的日记本在麦肯齐那里。"

"不得不承认，她表现得太可疑了，"克洛艾表示赞同，"不过，别担心，尼基，我确信，当我们不抱什么希望的时候，你的日记本会出现的。"

尽管刚刚发生了那些事情，但我心里仍然有种焦躁不安的感觉，总觉得麦肯齐没有她刚才装得那么无辜。

而现在呢，如果我的日记最后贴得洗手间的隔间到处都是，温斯顿校长也绝不会认为她有嫌疑。

麦肯齐就要毁了我的生活，还能逃脱惩罚，而我要阻止她却无能为力。

我真的不想承认这一点，但她确实彻头彻尾地陷害了我。而且是又一次的！！

我不小心把布里安娜一个人留在杂货店了！！啊啊啊！！！

自我提示

写日记有助于提高记忆力，所以，以后你可以把发生在你身上的事情全都记下来。

哦，我的天哪！我在麦片货架那儿看到布兰登的时候，我差点儿兴奋死了。我们注视着彼此，感觉像永远这样看下去。然后我们抓到了同一盒果味麦片，他竟然冲我笑了。我完全是晕晕乎乎地回到了家。现在回想起发生的那件事，我才意识到……

怪诞日记小贴士#12

不要忘记回忆哦！

今天早晨你早餐吃的什么？

你看到的最萌的衣服是什么样的？是谁穿的？

_____

_____

_____

_____

_____

_____

_____

_____

你今天听到的最好玩的事是什么？是谁跟你说的？

_____

_____

_____

_____

_____

_____

_____

_____

你最近听的一首歌是什么？

_____

_____

_____

_____

_____

_____

_____

_____

昨天晚上你做梦了吗？你梦到了什么？

_____

_____

_____

_____

_____

_____

_____

_____

你和别人通过电话吗？你们都说了些什么？

_____

_____

_____

_____

_____

_____

_____

_____

你在一天里说过最明智的话是什么？

_____

_____

_____

_____

_____

_____

_____

_____

_____

_____

图书馆，下午2:35

麦肯齐弄得我心烦意乱，我几乎都无法专心致志地把图书馆的书上架了。

我就知道我的日记本在她那儿。

但是与温斯顿校长在一起经历了那次超级尴尬的惨败之后，很显然，麦肯齐不会蠢到冒着被抓到的风险把我的日记本藏在她的包包里了。

但是如果麦肯齐没拿的话，谁拿了呢？！

我完全迷惘了！我感觉自己像要被一股绝望的潮水淹没了。

一想到我的日记本被到处传，每个人就像看最新版的校报一样看我的日记，我就觉得胃里翻江倒海。

谁想看尼基·马克斯韦尔的日记呀？到这里可以免费领取哟！

我眨眨眼睛，把眼泪憋回去，叹了一口气，然后注视着图书馆的窗外。因为我们的橄榄球队明天有一场比赛，他们正在球场上训练。

我想知道，他们当中会有多少人看我的日记，然后处心积虑让我的生活变得苦不堪言。午餐时间将会变得难以忍受！

我相当肯定，我们的四分卫明星布雷迪一定是主谋。不仅是因为他最近暗恋着麦肯齐，而且麦肯齐在生物课上给他发短信时还被抓了个现行……

就在这个时候，我犹如醍醐灌顶！

"哦，我的天哪！哦，我的天哪！克洛艾！佐伊！我想我知道谁拿了我的日记本啦！"

———————————————

男更衣室外面的走廊里，下午2:45

没门儿！我不可能那么做！

问我为什么？因为最后有人会挂掉的！这就是为什么！

挂掉的就是我！

克洛艾和佐伊想出了一个最疯狂的计划。而我非常肯定地知道：

1. 她们的计划绝对不会奏效。

2. 我们会被抓住。

3. 我们会被学校勒令停学。

然后我的父母会

杀了我！

而如果我死了，那我可能就永远都找不到我的日记本了！

我们三个都有浴室的通行证，所以我们现在应该在女生浴室里。

但不不不不不不是这样的！！

我们鬼鬼祟祟地在男更衣室的外面。主要是因为克洛艾、佐伊和我得出了全体一致的结论，我的日记本就在那里面。

它肯定在那里面！

我们认为，麦肯齐把日记本给了布雷迪，而他们相互发短信说的就是我的日记本。

因为那些球员现在正在球场上训练，布雷迪的背包应该在男储物柜的某个地方。

"我们现在要做的就是走进去，找到布雷迪放背包的那个柜子，然后拿出你的日记本！"佐伊在我们耳边非常大声地"窃窃私语"，她的声音好像在整个走廊里回荡，然后传进了教学楼这一边的每间教室。

"你疯了吗？！"我冲她发出"嘘"声，"我们被抓住怎么办？！"

"别担心啦！"克洛艾让我放心，"问问你自己吧，在这种情况下，你最喜欢的那本小说的女主角会怎么做。"

"是，对呀！"我喃喃地说，"那我星期五下午应该到哪儿去找舞会礼服，还有一群光着上身的狼人呢？我就那么一说！"

克洛艾冲我翻了个白眼。

克洛艾和佐伊在一直在努力地帮我找日记本，还有她们所做的一切，我真的非常感谢。但不得不承认，有时候我真的"严重"地为她俩发愁。

"刚刚过去的几分钟里，没人进进出出。"克洛艾小声地说，"我觉得那里面没什么人。"

"听着，小伙伴们，"我发话了，"我觉得我们应该在被那什么之前回到图书馆……"

"好哇！让我们跑着进去吧！"佐伊非常兴奋地说。

我还没来得及问一句"什么……"，克洛艾和佐伊就冲到男更衣室的大门，还把她们的脑袋探到里面。

"哦，我的天哪！克洛艾艾艾艾艾——佐伊伊伊伊——不——"我撕心裂肺地尖声低语。

但是太迟了，我别无选择，只能跟在她们后面。

我、佐伊和克洛艾往男更衣室里面偷窥！！

哦，我的天哪！

真不敢相信，我真的在男更衣室了！那是一个方形的大房间，沿着三面墙一溜儿都是储物柜。

这可比女更衣室大多了，而且还

有一块区域，是一排男生上厕所用的东西。

克洛艾、佐伊和我迅速开始搜查里面的每个储物柜，一个接一个地搜查。

"快！"佐伊回头朝我们喊道，"门边贴着呢，10分钟后游泳队要在这儿开会，所以我们没有太多时间！"

我有一种惊慌失措，想尖叫着跑出去的想法，最终我克制住了这个来势汹汹的冲动。

我们几乎翻遍了整个房间，但没有运气。然后，就在我要打开倒数第二个储物柜的时候，我在一个背包上发现了布雷迪的名字。

"这个一无是处的傻瓜坏蛋！"我嘟囔着，一边分类翻检他背包里的东西。

我觉得《蜘蛛侠》连环画下面好像有一本小书。

我难掩兴奋。"克洛艾！佐伊！我找到啦！"我大声叫了起来。

她们都冲过来，围在我身边。

"得是个名副其实的浑球才会去偷女孩子的……《搞定各种场合的纸杯蛋糕》，烹饪书？"我气急败坏地说。我捧着眼前的这本书，惊呆了，万分失望。

那本书的封面上有一些纸杯蛋糕，装点得像小猫咪和小狗狗。我感觉它们甜甜的微笑就是在嘲笑我。

我的日记本还在那儿之外的某个地方！但我没有时间为这个残酷的事实悲伤了！

因为我听到一个男人低沉而洪亮的声音，伴随着沉重的脚步声，正向更衣室的大门过来。我提到过那是更衣室唯一的一扇门吗？

我的心狂跳不止。克洛艾和佐伊像被冻住了一样。

她们看看我，然后看向那个男的过来的方向，眼里满是惊恐。我们肯定没法活着走出那里了。

当一只长了很多毛的手把那扇门推开一半的时候，我们都恐惧地注视着，然后像被凝固了一样！

"你说我们明天比赛只有两辆车是什么意思？我专门预定了三辆车啊！我们队怎么可能只有一部分人去比赛？那我还不如取消了呢！不是，我没有取消。我是说……什么？我能不挂等一会儿吗？你有别的电话进来了？不，我不能等，我要三辆车！……"

那个家伙就在门道那儿打电话。我们还真是"幸运"，那可是一通非常长的电话。

就在这个时候，我看到了一个巨大的推车，上面堆满了脏兮兮的球服和器材，在大约10英尺远的地方。

"克洛艾！佐伊！"我低声说，又指了指。

她俩立刻明白了我的计划。分分钟我们仨就来到那辆推车边上。

我们迅速抓起球衣、球裤、头盔和鞋子，我们穿衣服的速度大概是我们这一辈子中最快的一次。而且非常及时！

看到我们穿着球衣站在那里，玩弄着我们的大拇指，"粗暴"教练罗林气得鼻孔都要冒烟了。

"这究竟是怎么回事？"他大声喊道，"为什么我还有三个队员在这里晃荡，像在等公交车呢？你有什么借口，克莱顿？"

他指着佐伊，她穿着一件背上写有"克莱顿"的球衣。佐伊浑身颤抖得非常厉害，头盔都发出嘎吱声。

"回答我！怎么啦，克莱顿？猫叼走了你的舌头？"

"人……人不是命运的囚徒，而只是他自己思想的囚徒，"她结结巴巴地说道，"富兰克林·罗斯福说的。"

罗林教练皱着眉头，注视着佐伊，就好像她刚才回答他的是瑞典语一样。

"真是胡说八道！你觉得这样很好玩吗？你们都给我绕着跑道跑20圈，再去冲个澡怎么样？现在，这样才好玩呢！"

有个人站在更衣室的门外，非常大声地清了清嗓子："教练，打扰一下……"

我、克洛艾、佐伊和罗林教练都

转过身，想看看那人是谁。

布兰登站在门廊里，脖子上挂着他的照相机。

哦，我的天哪！我差点儿当场就晕过去了！

"我来这儿是想拍张您的照片，在《年度最佳教练》的文章中使用。我在这个时间找您不合适吧？"

罗林教练站直了，重新恢复镇定。"没有没有，孩子。我只是在为我们明天的大型比赛重温一下比赛策略。"他撒谎说，"这些男生会告诉你，我向来管理严格，而这就是为什么我们从没输过的原因。任何人都无

法超越我，任何人都不能超越我！"罗林教练轻声笑着，开玩笑似的给了我肩膀一拳。

"哦！"我想都没想就哼哼了一声，"我说的是，'噢'！"我假装用非常深沉的男孩声音说道。

布兰登盯着我，然后将目光转向克洛艾，然后又盯着佐伊，似乎永无止境。

他摇了摇头，满腹怀疑地眨巴着眼睛。

我们就要露馅儿啦！

"嘿，咱们到外面去吧。你可以拍一些我运动中的照片。"罗林教练摆了一个老套的姿势，好像他正在把球传到前场一样。

"实际上……您介意我让这几个球员暂停练习吗？"布兰登问道，指着克洛艾、佐伊和我，"我，嗯……想为这篇文章采访一下他们，这样读者就会明白您是怎样一位，嗯……一位了不起的教练。"

"他是有史以来最了不起的教练！"

我用我那可怕的、低沉的男孩声音说道。

"他就是这样的人！"佐伊咕哝着说。

"是的，哥们儿，"克洛艾补充说，"他让我们做男孩该做的很酷的事情，比如打嗝，捶打东西，还有在奎兹奇斯比萨店的球池玩……"

我使劲踢了佐伊一下，让她闭嘴。很显然，克洛艾认识的唯一的男孩就是她的小弟弟，乔伊。

"好！"布兰登神经质地笑了起来，"那么……这样的话，教练，您觉得那样没问题吧？我一采访完罗林队，就给您拍照。"

"罗林队？我喜欢这个名字的发音。你需要采访多久就多久吧。你们准备吧，我要到球场上去。"

罗林教练使了个眼色，然后朝门外走去。

我们站在那儿，默不作声，直到那扇门在他身后关上。

"尼基、克洛艾、佐伊！你们在男更衣室里穿成橄榄球运动员干什么呀？"布兰登问。

"其实，我可以解释。"我摘下头盔，"我们在找我的日记本。我们认为麦肯齐可能把它给布雷迪了。于是我们决定检查一下他的背包。"我羞愧地低下头，"可是我错了，日记本不在他这里。"

"好吧，你们几个最好赶快离开

这儿！趁教练还没想起那些事情，回来找你们。"

"谢谢你救了我们一命。"佐伊说道。

"不客气。尼基，希望你能找到日记本。"

布兰登冲我真诚地笑了，那种微笑常常会让我的心像冰棍一样融化。

但是，考虑到我的人生已经完蛋的事实，我只挤出了一丝微笑。"谢谢你，布兰登。真的非常感谢你帮我们摆脱了这个乱摊子。"我说。

但是在我的内心里我觉得所有的希望都破灭了。

我再也不想让我的朋友和我自己出演这样的"剧情"了。

致未来的我自己：

亲爱的未来的我，

如果你正读到这里，可能我已经被麦肯齐公开羞辱，并被驱逐到太平洋一个无名的小岛上。

尽管现在我是一个怪隐士，但是请告诉布里安娜，仍然不许她进我的房间，我希望你和布兰登事事都顺利。

爱你们的

尼基·马克斯韦尔

附：请把这本日记烧掉，这样别人都看不到了。

自我提示

关于日记，最精彩的部分之一是你能回首自己在几年、几个月、几星期、几天甚至几小时前说过的所有的傻话。人们通常从过去开始一页一页地读。

但是如果你仔细想想，一本日记几乎就像一台时光机器，记录着你的过去和未来！

那怎么做呢？

你可以给未来的自己写一封信，然后过段时间回过头来再读！

很怪吧，嗯哼？

但是非常酷！

怪诞日记小贴士#13

和未来的你自己成为笔友！

亲爱的未来的我：

你想对18岁的自己说些什么呢？给18岁的你自己写一封信吧。

亲爱的18岁的我：

_____
_____
_____
_____

谨上

_____岁的我

我，躲在秘密的地方悄悄写日记！

自我提示

写日记应该是一段愉悦的历程。只要有可能，就设法在一个安静的地方写日记，在那里你不会受打扰，也不会分心。

怪诞日记小贴士#14

找一个舒适的地方，

然后在你写日记的时候放松下来！

你会选择躲在什么秘密的地方悄悄写日记呢？

画一幅躲在秘密的地方悄悄写日记的画吧。

_____
_____
_____
_____
_____
_____
_____

家，下午4点

为什么？为什么？为什么我的生活这样糟糕透顶?!

我想我的日记本是永远地丢了。

尤其自从麦肯齐也在找我的日记本以来。

我曾在那个办公室发誓说我的日记本在她的包包里，但我想我错了。

我觉得她只是假装我的日记本在她那儿，这样一来我就会放弃，并停止寻找。让我完全出局会大大提高她真的找到我日记本的概率。

我知道这有点儿复杂。但是麦肯齐把每件事情都弄得很复杂。

我才不期待让整个学校都了解我个人的事情呢。

但是我猜想我会幸免于此。

就像我在这卑微而悲惨的生活中，已成功幸免了所有其他的重大灾难一样。

谢天谢地，我的两个闺密——克洛艾和佐伊一直给予我支持。

我依然无法相信，为了帮我找到日记本，她们竟然愿意冒着风险，去男生的更衣室之类的。

她们是史上最好的朋友！

家，下午4:30

现在，我感到神经刺痛，思绪纷乱。

我觉得开心，

生气，

如释重负，

又惴惴不安，

所有这些情感都在同一时间出现！

为什么呢？

我正在给自己搞一个巨大的同情派对，这时布里安娜放学跑着进来，用她最大的肺活量大声叫道："尼基！尼基！我有个大好消息！你绝对猜不到今天学校里发生了什么事情！"

我正在喝瓶装水，因为搞一个同情派对是一件让人筋疲力尽的事情，会让人又热又渴。

我实在是太震惊了，都不知道应

尼基，我们今天有展示介绍课！

咕咚咕咚

我在忙同情派对时稍作休息，

喝点儿瓶装水

我们所有小朋友都喜欢你日记本里那些好玩的画！

噗

"布里安娜，你把我的日记本带到学校去上展示介绍课啦?!"我大叫起来。

该是为她拿了我的日记本而冲她吼呢，还是应该谢她，因为她毕竟还了回来。但是以后我再也不必担心麦肯齐把我的日记一页一页贴得满学校都是，实际上那是一件不费脑子就能做到的事情。

我给了我那淘气的妹妹一个巨大无比的熊抱。

然后，我和布里安娜拉钩，让她保证绝对、永远都不再碰我的东西，除非事先征得我的同意。对于我们姐妹俩来说，这个小仪式是一种亲昵的体验，我几乎都要流泪了……

我拉钩同意并保证，

绝对不拿也不借用尼基的东西，

因为尼基会对我发飙，

她会一直批评我到第二天！

当然，作为一个"谎话精"，布里安娜完全否认是她拿走了我的日记本。

"是佩内洛普小姐偷了你那本讨厌的日记，才不是我呢！我叫她别那么做，但她根本就不听我的！"

那是布里安娜编的故事，而且她一直坚持那么说。

尽管如此，我想了想，佩内洛普小姐和麦肯齐还真有许多共同之处：

1. 她们两都超级烦人。

2. 她们俩都是大嘴巴。

3. 她们俩都爱抹厚厚的唇膏。

4. 她们都喜欢折磨我。

5. 她们都没什么脑子。

哦，我的天哪！她们很可能是同卵双胞胎，只是一出生就分开了！！

不过我得承认，我自己也不完美。

说真的，各位……

我就是这么个怪诞少女！！

自我提示

日记是一个会让人变得超级有创意的好地方。试着写一首诗，或者给原创歌曲填词。诗歌可以押韵，也可以是自由韵体（意思就是不押韵）。虽然这看起来可能是一项很难或很无聊的任务，但其实很简单，也很有趣！想想你最喜欢的说唱歌手或者说唱歌曲。说唱就是诗歌的另一种形式！

怪诞日记小贴士#15

如果你认为诗歌就是说唱音乐，那么写诗就像打个响指那么简单。

首先，你需要一个艺名。你可以在你自己的名字里加"MC"或"LIL"，或者编一些傻傻的东西。在下一页写下你创作的说唱歌曲、诗歌或者歌曲。嘿！你是一位诗人，只是你不知道而已。

_____
诗歌标题

_____

_____

_____

_____

_____

_____

_____

_____

_____

_____

_____

_____

_____

_____

_____

_____

_____

_____

_____

_____

_____

_____

_____

自我提示

你的日记属于你，而不是其他任何人的（不管你那淘气的妹妹会有什么想法）。所以呢，你可以写你的一天、你的暗恋对象、你最喜欢的东西、你想要举办的派对或者你想写的任何东西。任何时候你都可以写！

怪诞日记小贴士#16

你可以什么都写，

每件事都写，

或什么都不写

——你的日记你做主！

_____
*** 文
你的艺名

呃呃呃呃呃呃!翻开每页的角落,看看尼基的史努比"快乐舞蹈"吧。

作者简介：

　　蕾切尔·勒妮·拉塞尔是一位律师，相比于写法律文案，她更喜欢创作与少男少女有关的书籍（主要是因为这些书更有趣，睡衣与兔子拖鞋都是不允许出现在法庭陈述里的）。

　　她有两个女儿，喜欢跟她讨论一些话题。她的爱好包括种植紫色的花朵，做一些完全无用的手工（比如用冰棍、胶水与闪光的小东西制作一台微波炉）。蕾切尔现居弗吉尼亚州北部，养了一只约克夏宠物狗。这只宠物狗每天都要爬上她的电脑桌以此来威胁她，在她创作的时候用毛绒玩具扔她。没错，蕾切尔也认为自己是一个怪诞女！

This book is dedicated to YOU,

my wonderful readers!

Fill it with your daydreams,

drama, and doodles.

And always remember to let

your inner Dork shine through!

THIS DIARY BELONGS TO:

ME!!!

PRIVATE & CONFIDENTIAL

HEY, PEOPLE! NO PEEKING OR ELSE!! ☹

FRIDAY, AT HOME, 6:05 a.m.

OMG!!

I just had the most HORRIFIC nightmare!

The worst in my entire life!

I'm soooo FREAKED OUT I can barely write this.

ME, FREAKING OUT

I'm having cold sweats, my heart is pounding, and my brain is . . . numb with such intense . . . anguish it feels like it's about to, um . . . EXPLODE!

BOOM!

WHY?!

I DREAMED I LOST MY DIARY AT SCHOOL ☹!!!!!!

YES!! At SCHOOL!! Like, how CRAZY is THAT?!

The weird thing is that it seems like it actually happened. Because as soon as I woke up, all these detailed memories came flooding into my head, making me feel even more confused.

I can't imagine NOT writing in my diary! It's like I'm addicted or something.

In my dream I was so desperate that I found Brianna's old doodle book at the bottom of her toy box and started writing in that instead.

But mostly I was FRANTIC that someone would find my diary and read all the SUPERpersonal, SUPERembarrassing, SUPERsecret stuff about

AAAHHH!!

Me and ~~the~~ Princess
Sugar Plum Kissing all
the ~~cute~~ cute Baby uniCorns

♡ ♡

~~Me~~ Me →

♡

♡

BY: Brianna

That was me screaming.
WHY?
Because if I'm writing in
BRIANNA'S DOODLE BOOK, that can
mean only one thing...

I LOST MY
DIARY
AT SCHOOL
YESTERDAY ☹!!
AAAHHH!!!

AT HOME, 6:12 a.m.

I think I may be having a nervous breakdown or something because suddenly I just started crying and couldn't stop.

I WANT MY DIARY!!

My room was a total mess after just one box of tissues.

But by the time I sobbed my way through seven boxes of tissues, I looked like a giant

PLEASE. HELP. ME.

ME. BURIED BENEATH A HUGE MOUNTAIN OF 2,184 WADDED TISSUES

piece of LINT.

With EYEBALLS!

As much as I wanted to just lie there staring at the wall and sulking, I FINALLY decided it was time to drag my butt out of bed.

WHY?

Because all those wet, soggy tissues were quickly starting to dry and harden around my body, potentially transforming ME into a HUMAN piñata!!

And Brianna just LOVES piñatas.

I was absolutely TERRIFIED she would:

1. Dump six boxes of orange Tic Tacs down my throat.

2. String me up on a pole.

3. Smack me around with a plastic bat until I either burst or coughed up some candy.

That child has serious issues.

I'm just saying. . . ☹!!

AT HOME, 6:30 a.m.

I can't believe this is actually happening to me!

The last time I remember seeing my diary was yesterday at breakfast.

After I finished writing in it, I stuck it inside that cute little front zipper pocket of my backpack just like I always do.

I had a vocabulary quiz in French and a chapter test in geometry, so I didn't have time to write in it until my seventh-period class.

And when I opened the front zipper pocket of my backpack, my diary was GONE ☹!!!

Being the biggest dork in the entire school is bad enough. And now everyone is going to be reading my diary!

I'm WORSE than a TOTAL LOSER!!! I'm a

YUCKY Meatloaf Monster ☹

GRRRR!

BY BRIANNA

Okay! Is it just ME, or are these drawings a desperate cry for help?!

Brianna needs to be placed on a very potent antipsychotic medication. ASAP!

I'm just sayin' . . . !

* PLAN FOR FINDING MY LOST DIARY *

Step 1. Check the lost and found in school office. (If not found, proceed to Step 2.)

Step 2. Check each of my classrooms. (If not found, proceed to Step 3.)

Step 3. Check hallways, cafeteria, and library. (If STILL not found, proceed to Step 4.)

Step 4. Crawl inside my locker, slam the door shut, and . . .

DIE ☹!!

This whole fiasco is SO massively TRAUMATIZING I can barely think straight.

I'm sure I'm probably suffering from some very horrible and rare disorder like, um, Stress-Related Brain . . . Constipation!

And my illness will make it

HERB, THE JANITOR, DISCOVERS
THE
STANK COMING FROM LOCKER #724

nearly impossible for me to keep a diary.

At this point, the only thing I can do is use Brianna's doodle book to write very specific instructions to myself about HOW to keep a diary.

The good news is that anyone can use my personal tips to make their own diary.

Learning how to dork a diary will be both a thrilling and rewarding experience for all humankind.

And who knows, maybe one day your diary could even save your life. . .

HEY, KID! THIS IS A STICKUP! HAND OVER YOUR MOST VALUABLE POSSESSION, OR ELSE!

ME →

↖ MUGGER

UM, OKAY . . . !!!

WHACK!

—OW!

See what I mean?!

AM I NOT BRILLIANT ☺?!!

NOTE TO SELF

Your diary will probably become one of your most valuable possessions.

So it's important to determine which type of diary is best suited for your personality.

HOW TO DORK YOUR DIARY TIP #1

Discover your diary identity

Answer the following questions to find out the best type of diary for you.

1. It's a Saturday afternoon. Your homework is all done and you have an hour to do whatever you want. You decide to:

A. Play an exciting round of your favorite computer or video game.

B. Spend time relaxing by reading that new book your BFF has been raving about.

C. Check in with your friends via e-mail, text, or a social-networking site like Everloop.

D. Let your creative juices flow by drawing your favorite anime characters.

2. You left your diary in your third-hour English class, and your secret crush returns it to you during lunch. You:

A. E-mail him one of those cute animated thank-you e-cards and surprise him with his fave candy bar as a reward!

B. Gag on your meat loaf and then rush to the girls' bathroom, where you spend the rest of the day hiding out in a locked stall.

C. Hope he read the part in your diary about you liking him, so he'll finally ask you to the school dance. Hey, it's only a week away!

D. Blush profusely when he compliments that funky self-portrait in glitter you're working on for the art show and offer to draw a zany caricature of him as a thank-you.

3. When something is really bothering you, you usually:

A. Ponder the problem for an hour or two and then try to forget about it by doing a self-induced brain freeze with three gallons of Ben & Jerry's Chunky Monkey ice cream.

B. Privately obsess over the problem all day long while trying to convince everyone who asks "Are you okay?" that you're fine and nothing is bothering you because (1) your problem is way too complicated for them to understand, and (2) you're way too exhausted from pretending you're just fine to explain it to them.

C. Vent about the problem rather loudly to anyone and everyone who'll listen to you. Because if YOU ain't happy, NOBODY should be happy!

D. Distract yourself from worrying by channeling all that negative energy into a creative project. Like painting a still-life mural inside your locker and adding a water fountain, scented candles, and a yoga mat, and then totally chilling out in between classes.

4. Your birthday was three months ago and you still need to send your grandma a thank-you note for that hideous avocado-green sweater she knitted for you that was two sizes too big and more itchy than a severe case of poison ivy. You:

A. Drop her a quick e-mail sincerely telling her how you'll cherish her gift forever, while casually mentioning how much you really, really LOVE gift cards because one size fits all and they don't usually cause a rash.

B. Compose a heartfelt, handwritten thank-you note informing her that her gift is being worn almost daily. But you leave out the part about how you buried it out in the backyard and your dad accidentally found it when he was watering the grass and now it's his lucky bowling sweater.

C. Friend your grandma online and then post your thank-you note on her page along with a picture of yourself in the sweater SHE knitted so that her fourteen online friends can see it. But you also wear the ski mask YOU knitted so that your 1,784 online friends won't recognize you in a sweater that looks like dirty yak fur.

D. Paint a life-size portrait of

yourself wearing the sweater and send it to your grandma to show your gratitude. Because thanks to her, some very lucky dog or cat at the local animal shelter will give birth to her litter on a warm, fuzzy, two-sizes-too-big avocado-green sweater.

5. Which of the following is most true?

A. You're a very tech-savvy person. You're a team player and always up for a challenge.

B. You're friendly and a hopeless romantic. You love curling up in a comfy blanket and daydreaming.

C. You're happy and have lots of friends. There's always some type of drama going on in your life.

D. You're creative and enjoy art, music, drama, and poetry. Your personal style is unique and slightly edgy.

6. You hear the news that your BFF's soccer team just won the regional championship. You:

A. Send her the text message "You GO, GIRL! Congrats!"

B. Congratulate her with a big hug when you see her.

C. Leave her a phone message of you screaming hysterically.

D. Surprise her with a handmade poster on her locker that says "Congrats! You ROCK!"

7. You're about to wash your favorite pair of jeans and find ten dollars stashed in the back pocket from your last babysitting job. You're RICH! So you treat yourself to:

A. A ticket to that blockbuster movie based on your favorite book. You've been waiting, like, FOREVER for it to come out!

B. Gourmet CUPCAKES! SQUEEEEEE!!

C. Lip gloss! There's a buy-two-get-one-FREE sale at the mall!

D. Music for your iPod. There are some new tunes you've heard lately that are real ear candy.

8. You're at a slumber party and it's game time. Which of the following would you rather play?

A. Just Dance

B. The Game of Life

C. Truth or Dare

D. Pictionary

Now look back at which answer you circled for each question.

Which letter do you have the most of?

I have mostly._____

MOSTLY As

You are smart and curious, and you like learning new things. You will most enjoy keeping a diary on your computer. Write detailed entries about your interesting adventures and new discoveries.

MOSTLY Bs

You are kind and sensitive, and you like helping others. You will most enjoy writing in a diary or journal. Your dreams and feelings are sacred. Share them with your diary like a best friend.

MOSTLY Cs

You are friendly and outgoing, and you love people. You will most enjoy writing a blog. Select a fab online ID and share your exciting, DIVALICIOUS life with your friends.

MOSTLY Ds

You are creative and independent, and you are a talented artist. You will most enjoy keeping your thoughts in a sketchbook. Let your innermost feelings inspire you to create emo poetry, beautiful art, and hilarious doodles.

Now try out the suggested diary format for your personality. If you love it, you've found your match! However, if it's not the best fit, try the others and select the one you're most comfortable with.

GOOD LUCK ☺!

AT HOME, 7:10 a.m.

I'm already dreading school today.

Part of me wants to just give up and go back to bed. But since I desperately need to find my diary, staying home is NOT an option.

Just the thought of kids at my school reading my diary makes me physically ill. I was so nauseated this morning, I could barely even eat anything.

Of course, it didn't help that Brianna was making a huge gourmet breakfast for Miss Penelope.

SORRY! But Miss Penelope is JUST a stupid little HAND PUPPET! Any IDIOT could take one look at her and know she could NEVER eat that much food!!

But more than anything, I was totally GROSSED OUT by the nasty mess Brianna was making.

Why, why, why was I not born an only child ☹?!!

NOTE TO SELF

It's always fun to write about things that make you happy. But did you know that writing about a bad experience or disappointment can sometimes make you feel a lot better about the situation? If you're having a really cruddy day, remember to use your diary as a way to help you vent and work through your frustrations.

HOW TO DORK YOUR DIARY TIP #2

Write about the GOOD, the BAD, and the UGLY.

MISS PENELOPE SAYS, "YUMMY!!"

ME, TRYING REALLY HARD NOT TO THROW UP IN MY MOUTH!

THE GOOD:

← Me, the day I won first place in our school art show!!

Write about the BEST thing that has ever happened to you. How did you feel?

_____
_____
_____
_____
_____
_____

Draw a picture:
THE BEST THING
THAT EVER HAPPENED TO ME ☺!

Write about the WORST thing that has ever happened to you. How did you feel?

_____
_____
_____
_____
_____
_____

Draw a picture:
THE WORST THING
THAT EVER HAPPENED TO ME ☹!

THE BAD:

Me, after MacKenzie and Jessica ruined my brand-new party dress!

THE UGLY:

Me, caught on camera performing onstage with my little sister at the Queasy Cheesy pizza parlor!

Write about the most EMBARRASSING things that have ever happened to you. How did you feel?

_____
_____
_____
_____
_____
_____
_____
_____
_____

Draw pictures:

The TWO most embarRassing things that ever happened to me ☹!

NOTE TO SELF
Make sure you write in your diary every single day. Even if you LOSE your diary, just keep writing in a spare notebook or in your little sister's annoying doodle book.

ME AND MISS ~~PEALE~~ ~~PEALOPE~~ PENELOPE

SLURP ICE CREAM♥
BY ~~BRA~~ BRIANNA

ALWAYS DO THE WRITE THING.

Surprise! This is a POP QUIZ! Grab a pencil or pen and write a diary entry RIGHT NOW about what happened to you today! Keep writing until you see the word "STOP."

STOP

GIRLS' BATHROOM AT SCHOOL, 7:45 a.m.

As soon as I got to school, I practically ran to the office. I didn't even wait around for my BFFs, Chloe and Zoey.

The school secretary, Mrs. Pearson, was placing mail in the teacher mailboxes.

"Um. . . excuse me, but has anyone found a lost book?" I asked frantically.

"Good morning, Nikki. Actually, a student DID turn in a book yesterday! He said he found it in the hall near the cafeteria."

I could not believe my luck! I was so happy and relieved, I could have hugged her.

"OMG! Someone found it and turned it in?" I squealed excitedly. "I'm pretty sure it's MINE!"

Thank goodness this nightmare was finally over.

When Mrs. Pearson handed me the book, I took one look and my heart dropped.

It was NOT my diary!

I needed ANOTHER geometry

NOOOOO!!

book like I needed a hole in the head. Heck, I didn't understand the math problems in the book I already had.

"Um, thanks. But this ISN'T my book," I muttered, and handed it back to Mrs. Pearson.

"Well, take a look in the lost and found box. There's a chance it could be in there," she said encouragingly.

I closed my eyes and prayed it would be there.

Please let my diary be in the lost and found!

Please let my diary be in the lost and found!

Please let my diary be in the lost and found!

Then I sighed and walked over to a large cardboard box sitting in a corner.

I slowly opened it and carefully went through each and every item. . .

ME, SEARCHING FOR MY DIARY AMONG ALL THE VERY WEIRD ITEMS IN THE LOST AND FOUND

Princess Sugar Plum lunch box
Flea collar
Pet lizard
LOST 'N' FOUND
Chewed pencil
Moldy bologna sandwich
3-D glasses
Ortho retainer
Matted hair extension

But unfortunately, it was NOT in there.

I bit my lip and tried to blink back my tears.

"Don't worry, dear. It's bound to turn up later today," Mrs. Pearson said, trying to make me feel better. "And to make sure we find it, I'm going to post a note alerting all my student office assistants to keep an eye out for a book belonging to Nikki Maxwell! Okay?"

That's when my knees got weak and my stomach felt so queasy I thought I was going to throw up.

But it WASN'T because of the moldy bologna sandwich.

Or the dirty ortho retainer.

Or the matted hair extension (which was quite disgusting in a peculiar sort of way).

I suddenly realized my little diary problem was probably going to get a lot WORSE before it got better.

WHY?!

Because JESSICA HUNTER is a student OFFICE ASSISTANT!

And Jessica's BFF is MACKENZIE HOLLISTER!

And everyone knows that MacKenzie Hollister

HATES MY GUTS!!

Even if at some point my diary IS turned in to the lost and found, there's a VERY good chance MacKenzie is going to intercept it, read it, and then plaster pages around the school— just to make my life more miserable than it already is. And there's nothing I can do about it.

Except rush straight to the girls' bathroom and have a massive mental meltdown. . .

AAAAAAHHH☹!!

(That was me screaming, AGAIN!)

NOTE TO SELF

**NOTE TO SELF
WARNING:**

Unfortunately, parents, bratty kid sisters and brothers, friends, enemies, and even total strangers LOVE to read diaries that do NOT belong to them.

HOW TO DORK YOUR DIARY TIP #4

NEVER, EVER LEAVE YOUR DIARY WHERE A NOSY CREEP CAN SNEAK A PEEK!

If someone caught you writing in your diary, what would you say to trick them? Write four different responses below:

OMG, NIKKI!
YOU'RE WRITING
IN A DIARY?
CAN I READ IT?

OH, THIS? IT'S JUST
A . . . BOOK
I GOT FROM MY
DOCTOR ON, UM . . .
TOENAIL ODOR.

HEY! IS THAT YOUR DIARY?!

Never let anyone tell you that keeping a diary is a silly or childish thing to do. Reflecting on your feelings and experiences is actually a very mature activity. If someone said something rude about you having a diary, what would your response be?

ONLY DORKS HAVE DIARIES!

How would you disguise your diary? Draw phony book covers on the next two pages:

PHONY BOOK COVER #1

PHONY BOOK COVER #2

ENGLISH CLASS, 8:00 a.m.

I was completely out of breath by the time I arrived at my first class.

I frantically checked around my desk, on the counters, and on the bookshelves. But there was no sign of my diary ☹! I was like, JUST GREAT!

I collapsed into my seat, closed my eyes, and massaged my temples, trying to replay yesterday's events in my mind.

If I had somehow lost my diary, WHO would have been around me to find it? I suspiciously eyeballed all the potential suspects in my classroom.

That's when I remembered that Chloe walked with me to class yesterday. As usual, she was raving nonstop about the latest novel she'd just finished. It was called . . .

"OMG, Nikki! It is the BEST book EVER! I could NOT stop reading it.

"This talented artist is obsessed with drawing this supercute guy she had made up in her mind. Then one day he shows up at her school as a new student. And he can read her thoughts.

"The doodle dude seems really nice until her crush, Hunk Finn, an even cuter guy in her art class, sketches her for a class project and shares a double-fudge chocolate cupcake with her.

"When Doodle Dude starts acting scary jealous, the artist decides she has no choice but to secretly erase all her drawings to get rid of him.

"Then she totally freaks out when Doodle Dude steals ALL her erasers so she can't erase him. And then he starts eating paper to gain superpowers and immortality.

"Nikki, since you're an artist too, I think you're gonna LOVE it!"

I was like, "Um, thanks, Chloe. Can't wait!"

Then she handed me her Deadly Doodle Dude book, and I

unzipped my backpack and stuck it inside.

That was probably when my diary accidentally fell out...

AND CHLOE FOUND IT ☹?!

I have to admit, Chloe is hopelessly obsessed with romance novels.

And she'll read just about ANYTHING. Soup can labels. Lip gloss tubes.

What if she picked up my DIARY, read it, and LOVED, LOVED, LOVED all the wacky drama?!

I know this might sound really crazy. . . ! But what if Chloe

actually turned my very private, dorky tales of WOE into a bestselling book series?!

AND a blockbuster Hollywood movie?!

Without even telling me?!!

I'd probably NEVER, EVER get over it. My life would be totally RUINED.

And then, many years later, Chloe and I might just happen to see each other on the street. . .

NIKKI, DAH-LING! I WOULDN'T BE FAMOUS AND FILTHY RICH IF I HADN'T FOUND YOUR DIARY. PLEASE, LET ME AT LEAST DROP A QUARTER IN YOUR LITTLE CUP!

I WILL WORK FOR FOOD

ME

CHLOE

Hey, it could happen! Why is my life so hopelessly CRUDDY?!

NOTE TO SELF

Keeping a diary isn't just about describing what kind of person you are.

It's also about DISCOVERING

what kind of person you are.

That's why it's important to dig deep and examine your thoughts and feelings. Be very comfortable with writing about YOU!

HOW TO DORK YOUR DIARY TIP #5

IT'S ALL ABOUT ME, MYSELF, AND I.

If you can answer each and every one of the following questions, you'll be on your way to keeping an AWESOME diary.

What makes you really happy?

_____

_____

_____

What makes you really sad?

_____

_____

_____

_____

_____

_____

What's your biggest life accomplishment?

_____

_____

_____

_____
_____
_____
_____
_____
_____
_____
_____
_____

_____
_____
_____
_____
_____
_____
_____
_____
_____

What are you most proud of?

_____
_____
_____
_____
_____
_____
_____
_____
_____
_____
_____
_____
_____

What's your biggest fear?

_____
_____
_____
_____
_____
_____
_____
_____
_____
_____
_____
_____
_____

What's your biggest embarrassment?

_____
_____
_____
_____
_____

Who's your biggest hero?

_____
_____
_____
_____
_____

What do you want to be when you grow up?

What are three of your favorite movies?

What are three of your favorite TV shows?

Who are three of your favorite pop stars?

What are three of your favorite books?

_____

What's your favorite food?

_____

What are three of your favorite songs?

_____

What's your least favorite food?

_____

Who's your best friend in the world?

Where do you like to hang out?

Who are you hopelessly crushing on?

FRENCH CLASS, 9:50 a.m.

HELP!! Today is turning into the WORST day EVER!

Right before French class I decided to search all the girls' bathrooms for my missing diary.

And guess who I ran into?!

HINT: She was looking in the mirror, slathering on seventeen layers of Fluorescent Candy Apple Bliss lip gloss.

You guessed it!

MACKENZIE HOLLISTER!!

And get this! She was actually NICE to me.

Which, of course, made me SUPERsuspicious.

Especially when she bumped into me and then tried to act all innocent and apologetic, like the whole thing was just an accident.

"Oopsie! I just bumped into you, Nikki. But it was totally an accident. Sorry! I hope you'll accept my apology. By the way, does this lip gloss match my shoes?"

I could NOT believe my ears. How dare MacKenzie apologize for being a clumsy ox AND ask me for fashion advice, all in the same breath! Where did that girl learn her manners? Doggie obedience school? I'm just sayin'!

Anyway, as soon as I left the bathroom, I noticed everyone in the hall was pointing and laughing at me.

And I didn't have the slightest idea why.

Well,

SURPRISE, SURPRISE!

MacKenzie had given me a little, um, PRESENT. . .

ME, BEING PUBLICLY HUMILIATED BY MACKENZIE'S LITTLE PRANK

GIRLS

When I saw her again in French class, I had to restrain myself from sneaking off to the girls' bathroom to borrow a roll of toilet paper.

WHY?

Because a very dark and evil side of me wanted to TP her butt right there in the middle of class.

ME, GIVING MACKENZIE A LITTLE TASTE OF HER OWN MEDICINE!

EVIL ME

Anyway, I was a little surprised when she sashayed over to my desk.

"I heard from a very reliable source that you lost your little diary. It would be horrible if all your secrets got out. So I have some important news for you!"

My mouth dropped open and my heart skipped a beat. OMG!! MacKenzie knew my diary was missing?!

Had she found out from Jessica ALREADY? My worst NIGHTMARE was coming true!

And I had a really bad feeling about her news.

"Actually, MacKenzie, it would be news to me if, for once, you DIDN'T stick YOUR nose in MY personal business."

That's when she stared right at me with her icy blue eyes.

I'M GOING TO SEARCH THIS ENTIRE SCHOOL UNTIL I FIND YOUR DIARY. AND WHEN I DO, YOU'LL BE SORRY!

I'M ALREADY SORRY! SORRY YOUR BREATH SMELLS LIKE YOU HAD FRANKS' N'BEANS FOR BREAKFAST!

She glared at me, stuck her nose in the air, and then sashayed back to her desk.

I just HATE it when MacKenzie sashays!

But now I have just TWO nagging questions:

1. WILL SHE FIND MY DIARY BEFORE I DO?

2. IF SHE DOES, WHAT EVIL, CRUEL, AND DIABOLICAL PLAN DOES SHE HAVE IN

STORE FOR ME? ☹!!

It's hard to concentrate on my French lesson with MacKenzie eyeballing me all evil-like from across the room.

I swear! That girl is going to be really sorry when

ME AND MAX the ~~ROACH~~ ROACH

GO FOR A WALK

&Y ♥
Brianna

Did I just see Max the Roach on a. . . LEASH?!

Okay, I give up!

There is no question about it. . .

I'M DOOMED!! ☹!!

NOTE TO SELF

You never know if your diary might fall into the wrong hands. Just in case, make sure you have codes that only YOU understand!

HOW TO DORK YOUR DIARY TIP #6

WHEN NECESSARY, GO INTO SECRET-CODE MODE.

Chloe and Zoey and I always talk about the CCP (Cute, Cool & Popular) crowd and GGG-ing (giggling, gossiping, and glossing). Make a list of codes you and your friends have and what they all mean.

_____

_____

_____

_____

_____

_____

_____

_____

_____

_____

_____

_____

_____

You could also come up with new meanings for these abbreviations, and then no one will be able to crack your code!

WCD = Westchester Country Day OR World-Class Dork OR:

_____

_____

_____

_____

_____

_____

_____

_____

_____

_____

LOL = Laughing Out Loud OR Laughing Obnoxiously Loud OR:

_____

_____

_____

_____

BRB = Be Right Back OR Busy
Rescuing Batman OR:

_____

_____

_____

_____

_____

_____

_____

_____

_____

_____

BTW = By the Way OR:

_____

_____

_____

_____

_____

_____

_____

_____

_____

_____

_____

OMG = Oh My God OR:

_____

_____

_____

_____

_____

_____

_____

_____

CCP = Cute, Cool & Popular
OR:

_____

_____

_____

_____

_____

_____

_____

RCS = Roller-Coaster Syndrome
OR:

_____

_____

_____

_____

_____

_____

_____

TTYL = Talk to You Later OR:

_____

_____

_____

_____

_____

_____

JK = Just Kidding OR:

_____

_____

_____

_____

_____

_____

_____

Although you'll spend a lot of time writing in your diary, you can also express yourself through art.

Try adding DRAWINGS, DOODLES, CARTOONS, and COMIC STRIPS. They can be serious, artsy, emo, or just plain silly. If you're a supertalented artist, create a masterpiece. Or try drawing simple stick people. Or trace your hand and make it into a turkey like you did back in kindergarten. Just have FUN!

HOW TO DORK YOUR DIARY TIP #7

RELEASE YOUR INNER ARTIST!

Here is a four-panel comic strip called "My Diary Drama." (A panel is just another name for the box the artwork is placed inside.)

Now you're going to make your own four-panel comic strip! But before you get started, plan what it is going to be about.

My comic strip is called:

_____

_____

_____

_____

PANEL 1

Panel 1 will contain a picture of:

_____

_____

_____

_____

The characters are saying:

_____

_____

_____

_____

PANEL 2

Panel 2 will contain a picture of:

_____

_____

_____

The characters are saying:

_____

_____

_____

_____

PANEL 3

Panel 3 will contain a picture of:

_____

_____

_____

_____

_____

The characters are saying:

_____

_____

_____

_____

_____

PANEL 4

Panel 4 will contain a picture of:

_____

_____

_____

_____

_____

The characters are saying:

_____

_____

_____

_____

Now you're ready to draw your own comic strip in the space provided. Have fun ☺!

SOCIAL STUDIES CLASS, 10:47 a.m.

I'm beginning to think my situation is HOPELESS!

I've checked all the halls, the library, and the cafeteria. AND I just scoured my social studies classroom.

But still no trace of my diary ☹!!

That's when I started wondering if maybe someone picked it up by accident.

Who, other than Chloe, did I come in close contact with yesterday?

Well, that's a no-brainer! The answer is . . . ZOEY!!

As library shelving assistants, Chloe, Zoey, and I go to the library during study hall. We gather up all the library books and place them back on their proper shelves.

I have to admit, I don't exactly remember whether or not I even had my diary in the library yesterday. But what if I DID . . . ?!

OMG! What if Zoey accidentally grabbed my diary while she was

ZOEY ACCIDENTALLY GRABBING MY DIARY!!

gathering that huge stack of books?

And what if while she was putting them back on the shelves, she found my diary and READ IT?! She'd have enough drama to launch her own TV talk show. . .

Let's TALK
with ZOEY FRANKLIN

ME

GULP!

BACK AGAIN TODAY IS NIKKI, TO SHARE MORE ABOUT HER AMAZINGLY PATHETIC LIFE!

Right now I'm so utterly frustrated, I feel like crying.

But mostly I have this very sick feeling deep down in my gut that I'll probably never see my diary again.

I can't believe this is happening to me!

☹!!

 **NOTE TO SELF**
A diary can be a great place to figure out your future goals in life. Make some of them short-term goals that you can achieve in a month or less. And make some of them long-term goals that may take a year or more to achieve.

Remember to keep track of the ones you've accomplished and set exciting new ones.

HOW TO DORK YOUR DIARY TIP #8

Dare to dream about your future!

List three things you'd like to accomplish.

Tomorrow:

_____

_____

_____

_____

Next week:

_____

_____

_____

_____

Next month:

_____

_____

_____

_____

Next year:

_____

_____

_____

_____

I had barely gotten out onto the gym floor when both Chloe and Zoey came rushing over.

"Hey, Nikki!" Chloe said, looking a bit worried. "We waited for you by your locker this morning, and again after second period. We started thinking maybe you were at home sick or something."

"Yeah, we're glad to see you," said Zoey. "Although, to be honest, you DO look a little down today. Are you okay?" she asked, giving me a big hug.

I do NOT deserve friends like Chloe and Zoey!

Why did I EVER suspect that my BFFs would find my diary, read it, and then share it with the entire world? I could trust them with my LIFE!

A wave of guilt washed over me. That's when I decided to tell Chloe and Zoey what happened.

I lowered my voice to barely a whisper.

I could NOT believe Chloe and Zoey just screamed it out loud in front of the ENTIRE gym class

ACTUALLY, I AM A LITTLE DOWN. I THINK I, UM, LOST MY . . . D–DIARY!!

?!!   ?!!

YOU LOST YOUR DIARY?!

like that!

EVERYONE heard it and started staring at us.

"SHHHHHHHHHHH!!"

I whisper-shouted. "I was hoping to keep it a secret! BTW, did I mention that MacKenzie knows my diary is missing? She's looking for it too."

"Not good!" Chloe said, scrunching up her face like she smelled something really bad.

"Well, girlfriends, I guess that just means WE have to find it before Miss Thang does!" Zoey said, putting her hands on her hips.

"Yeah! And MacKenzie and her CCPs are no match for the three of us! Right?" Chloe said, giving me jazz hands.

I was so overcome with emotion, I started to choke up right in the middle of my jumping jacks.

If my diary is anywhere in this school, my BFFs, Chloe and Zoey, are definitely the ones to help me find it.

Maybe things aren't so hopeless after all.

☺‼

NOTE TO SELF
Your diary is a good place to remind yourself that things aren't always as bad as you think. You can use it to plan exciting events and fun activities. Feeling down? Cheer yourself up by throwing a party and inviting all your friends!

HOW TO DORK YOUR DIARY TIP #9

DON'T BE A PARTY POOPER! HAVE FUN CELEBRATING

YOU!

Complete the following exercise:

IT'S MY PARTY‼

SURPRISE! You are throwing yourself a really big party because you deserve it.

What kind of party will it be?

☐ costume party
☐ slumber party
☐ pool party
☐ dance party
☐ scavenger hunt
☐ _____
  fill in the blank

Where will it be located?

_____

_____

_____

What foods will be served?

_____

_____

_____

_____

MY PARTY GUEST LIST

FRIENDS(Make a list of ten friends you'd invite to your party.)

_____

_____

_____

_____

SPECIAL GUESTS
(Make a list of ten people you'd invite to your party who are alive or dead: people from history; characters from your favorite books, movies, or TV shows; celebrities; pro athletes; etc.)

_____

_____

_____

_____

_____

CAFETERIA, 12:25 p.m.

I slumped over my lunch like a zombie. The rotting casserole smell didn't even bother me.

"It's like my diary disappeared into thin air," I muttered. "I have no clue how I lost it. How can I be so dense?"

Zoey squeezed my shoulder sympathetically. "Don't beat yourself up, Nikki. Besides, three heads are better than one. Let's all try to remember if you had it during lunch yesterday. We'll start with the moment we sat down to eat."

"Hmmm." Chloe scratched her head, crossed her eyes, and clicked her tongue. She only did this when she was really deep in thought. I could almost hear the squeaky cogs in her brain turning. "Yesterday at lunch?"

"Well, Zoey opened her apple juice and took a sip. Then I said, 'Nikki, are you going to eat that fry?' And Nikki said, 'I was until you picked it up, sniffed it, and asked me if I was going to eat it.' Then I said, 'Thanks for the fry!' Then I asked Zoey if I could have a bite of her mom's famous blueberry muffins, 'cause those things are crazy delicious. And Zoey said—"

"Um, Chloe, how about we just skip all the tiny details?" I said, trying my best to remain calm.

"Well, to be honest, I don't exactly remember whether or not you had your diary with you at lunch yesterday," Chloe admitted. "But I DO remember the time you accidentally threw it in the trash when you dumped your tray."

Zoey's eyes lit up. "Wow! Chloe has a good point. If it happened once, it could happen again. Nikki, maybe . . . you tossed it!"

"OMG! You guys think I threw my diary away?! What if I DID?!" I groaned.

That's when I jumped up from the lunch table.

"Come on, guys, we only have

MY DIARY?!

ME, ACCIDENTALLY THROWING AWAY MY DIARY AT LUNCH??!!

thirteen minutes before lunch is over."

"Where are we going?" Chloe asked.

"To the Dumpster!" I yelled over my shoulder.

"You've got to be kidding me!" Zoey made an ick face.

"The good news is that MacKenzie would NEVER think to look there!" I felt hopeful again.

Chloe and I sprinted across the cafeteria toward a back door that led outside as Zoey lagged behind.

"Personally, I don't think MacKenzie wants to read your diary THAT badly," Zoey grumped.

As we approached the Dumpster, the stench of three-day-old fish sticks and spoiled milk almost knocked me over.

But I was desperate.

So I just gritted my teeth, held my breath, and cautiously peered inside.

"I'm in my happy place! I'm in my happy place! I'm in my happy place!" Zoey chanted as she climbed in.

She was doing one of her goofy meditation exercises, but it was so not working.

"You know this garbage is crawling with disease-laden bacteria, right?" nagged Zoey. "When I get home, I'm going to take off these clothes and burn them!"

Chloe was already inside, busily digging through the rubbish.

ME, CHLOE, AND ZOEY SEARCHING FOR MY DIARY IN THE DUMPSTER

But do you wanna know the really FREAKY part?

She actually seemed to be enjoying it!

"If my diary is in here, it will probably be toward the top," I said, swatting at an overly friendly fly.

Unfortunately, all I could find amid the rotten food were broken hockey sticks and flat basketballs from gym class, and test papers with big fat red Fs on them. None of them were mine, I swear!

"Hey! Check it out!" Chloe shouted happily.

"OMG! You found my diary?!" I asked excitedly.

"Not yet, but isn't this floppy hat really cute?" She put on the hat and struck a pose. "Now I look like a celebrity!"

"It's nice, but we gotta keep looking," I huffed.

A minute later I heard a high-pitched "SQUEEEE!!" It was Chloe. Again!

"What?! What?!" I asked eagerly.

"OMG! It's the newest issue of Vampire Hunks Monthly!"

She held the magazine to her chest and hugged it.

"How could anyone toss this? Finders keepers!"

"Come on, Chloe!" Zoey said, rolling her eyes. "Be serious!"

"I'm searching, already. Sheesh!" Chloe pushed a garbage bag aside and bent down to pick up something.

"OH. MY. GAWD!" she screeched.

I sighed. "Please tell me it's my diary this time."

"It's a Hug-Me-Harry bear!" She gave the dirty teddy bear a squeeze. "I'm keeping him."

"Just great!" I mumbled, looking at my watch, which was covered in a thick layer of mustard. "Lunch is almost over, and we've barely scratched the surface here. I don't know if I'll EVER find my diary."

I crawled out of the Dumpster.

Defeated. And really, really smelly.

"Hey! I know just what will cheer you up, " Chloe cooed in a very annoying, high-pitched baby voice. "How about a big fat HUGGY-WUGGY!"

Then she shoved Dirty Harry right in my face.

I was like, OH. NO. SHE. DIDN'T!!

Chloe must have totally lost her mind.

And Zoey wasn't helping matters by giggling like a hysterical chipmunk.

But since they are my BFFs, I decided NOT to get an attitude about the whole thing.

So . . . I just hugged the stupid bear.

I'm ashamed to actually admit it, but Hug-Me-Harry DID make me feel a little bit better. Once I got past the odor. ☺!!

NOTE TO SELF

Sometimes the most insignificant things can spark the best memories. Save your ticket stub from that fabulous live concert or that blockbuster movie. Keep the hilarious note your BFF passed to you during math class. Hang on to that cute doodle you did of your crush on the back of your lunch napkin. You can use your diary as a place to keep little things that you cherish.

BRANDON

HOW TO DORK YOUR DIARY TIP #10

TREASURE YOUR TRASH.

Find two things that bring back great memories.

Tape the first one in the space below.

Now make a note about what you taped on the last page and how you got it, so you won't ever forget.

_____

_____

_____

_____

_____

_____

_____

_____

_____

_____

_____

_____

_____

_____

_____

_____

_____

_____

_____

Now tape the second item here and write about it below.

_____

_____

_____

_____

_____

_____

_____

_____

_____

_____

_____

_____

_____

_____

_____

_____

_____

_____

_____

_____

BIOLOGY CLASS, 1:30 p.m.

Today is turning out to be the longest school day EVER.

PLEASE, PLEASE, PLEASE

let it end soon.

I don't know how much more I can take.

By the time I got to biology class, it seemed like the ENTIRE school was gossiping about my lost diary ☹!! I seriously considered just faking a headache and going home early.

I tried my best to ignore all the stares and whispers in the classroom. But it was really hard to do with MacKenzie sitting across the room gossiping about me right to my face.

I was in such a grumpy mood, I barely said hi to my crush, Brandon. Even though he gave me a big smile and told me he had something important to give me

after class.

Sorry, but the last thing I needed right then was another extra-credit project. In spite of the fact that it usually meant us spending an extra hour working together in the lab.

Even though our school has a very strict policy about no cell phones in class, I watched in utter amazement (and with slight envy) as MacKenzie sat there texting away like there was no tomorrow. All while our teacher, Ms. Kincaid, drew diagrams of molecules on the board and droned on and on about the day's massively boring lesson on microbiology.

It was very sad but true: MacKenzie could get away with

murder! And everyone at WCD, even the teachers, seemed to just look the other way.

Or so I thought.

"ADP is a molecule formed from ATP by the breaking off of a phosphate group. It results in a release of energy that is used for biological reactions and— Miss Hollister, you seem really busy with your cell phone while I'm up here in front of the class trying to teach. I hope I'm not disturbing you?"

I could NOT believe our teacher actually said that!

It got so quiet in the room, you could hear a pin drop. Everyone in the class, including the teacher, was staring at MacKenzie.

But girlfriend was so busy texting that she didn't even notice.

Frustrated, Ms. Kincaid raised her voice. "Miss Hollister! Would you PLEASE put down your phone! Now!"

Apparently, MacKenzie didn't hear a single word.

Highly irritated, Ms. Kincaid walked up and stood right next to her.

MISS HOLLISTER!!

SNATCH!

But MacKenzie was so absorbed that she kept right on texting.

That's when . . .

OMG! It was SO funny!

MacKenzie almost jumped out of her seat.

And Ms. Kincaid actually confiscated her cell phone.

The entire class cracked up, and for a split second I felt a little sorry for MacKenzie.

But she totally had it coming!

"MacKenzie, you know the rules. We have zero tolerance for cell phone use in class. I'll return it to you in ten days, AFTER I receive a five-page paper on why cell phones should not be allowed in class. Do you understand?"

MacKenzie looked like she was going to DIE of embarrassment. "I g-guess so!" she stammered.

"And since your message is SO

important you've interrupted our class time, I think it's only fitting that it be shared with ALL of us."

MacKenzie looked absolutely LIVID.

Ms. Kincaid squinted at the phone and read the last message aloud.

"From Brady Grayson: No, that's way too risky. I have an early football practice today, but I can give it back to you afterward. Meet me in the gym at three o'clock."

The class snickered loudly.

With MacKenzie sufficiently mortified, the teacher resumed her lecture.

"Now, where was I? . . . ADP, I think. ADP is a molecule formed from ATP by the breaking off of a phosphate group. . ."

After class was over, I had no intention of sticking around.

"Hey, wait! I want to give you something!" Brandon said, reaching for his bag.

"Actually, I'm supposed to be meeting Chloe and Zoey right now. . ."

"It'll only take a minute. I heard that you lost your journal. So until you find it, I wanted to

give you this. . ."

Brandon handed me a thin, square package wrapped in notebook paper.

I opened it and was supersurprised to see it was a spiral notebook.

"It's nothing fancy. I just had a couple extra ones lying around in my locker. I figured you'd put it to good use."

I just stared at him, speechless.

It was one of the sweetest gifts anyone has ever given me. Lately.

"Th-thanks, Brandon!" I sputtered, blushing like crazy. "It's a really nice . . . color! And it has two hundred and fifty-six pages and cost three seventy-nine. I mean, wow!"

He smiled and blushed too. "I'm glad you like it."

"Yeah, I do. A lot!"

"Um, I guess I'll see you

tomorrow, then."

"Yep, same here!"

"Bye!"

"Bye! Thanks again!"

I placed the notebook in my backpack and walked out of class.

But in my head I was doing my Snoopy "happy dance."

After which, I had an obligatory attack of RCS (roller-coaster syndrome). OMG! It felt like I had a thousand butterflies fluttering around in my stomach. WHEEEEEEEEEEEE! ☺!!

NOTE TO SELF

Do you sometimes want to say stuff out loud and speak your mind, but you're a little nervous or afraid?

Although you don't want to be rude, it can be good to tell people exactly what you think and how you feel. Otherwise, you end up saying it inside your head so no one else hears it but you. And after a while that will get kind of old.

HOW TO DORK YOUR DIARY TIP #11

WRITE DOWN ALL THE STUFF YOU ONLY SAY INSIDE YOUR HEAD.

WHAT I SAID ALOUD . . .

HOW ABOUT TEN DOLLARS TO WASH MY VAN?

UMM... OK.

WHAT I SAID INSIDE MY HEAD . . .

WASH IT?!
LET'S
SELL IT!!

SURE, DAD!
AS LONG AS
I CAN WEAR
A BAG OVER
MY HEAD!

What are some of the things you've only said inside your head, but that you've thought about saying to:

1. Your BFFs?

_____

_____

_____

_____

_____

_____

_____

_____

_____

_____

_____

2. Someone at school who isn't always supernice to you?

_____

_____

_____

_____

_____

_____

_____

_____

_____

_____

_____

_____

_____

_____

_____

3. Your parents?

5. Your crush?

4. Your siblings?

GEOMETRY CLASS, 2:00 p.m.

AAAHHH ☹!!

That was me screaming.

I CANNOT believe I just made a

TOTAL FOOL of myself!!

Chloe, Zoey, and I decided to check the lost and found again between classes.

Mainly because Jessica is now the sixth-hour office assistant, and we wanted to get to it before she did.

When we walked in, we saw two girls sitting on the floor behind the counter, frantically tossing items back into the lost and found box.

We were NOT the least bit surprised to see it was **MACKENZIE** and **JESSICA.**

EW! ICK!

LOST 'N' FOUND

They both seemed a little startled to see us standing there.

MacKenzie quickly grabbed her purse and zipped it up. "Jess, thanks for helping me find . . . my . . . um, lip gloss. I'll see you in class."

Jessica walked up to the counter and gave us her biggest phony smile. "Hi there. May I help you?"

There was no way I was going to discuss my personal business with HER. "Is Mrs. Pearson in?"

"Actually, no. She'll be back from a meeting in about ten minutes. Is there something I can help you with?" she said, glancing at MacKenzie while trying her best not to snicker.

"I hope you haven't lost anything really important," MacKenzie snarled. "You know. Like a diary with a pocket on the cover. Don't waste your time checking the lost and found, because it's definitely NOT here! Right, Jessica?"

Chloe, Zoey, and I could NOT believe she actually said that to our faces.

There was now no doubt whatsoever in my mind that

MacKenzie had found my diary. I was sure it was probably stuffed in her purse.

"MacKenzie, I want my diary back," I said, looking right into her beady little eyes.

"Yeah! Hand it over!" Chloe huffed.

"Right NOW!" Zoey growled.

MacKenzie just flipped her hair and glared at us.

I DON'T HAVE THE SLIGHTEST IDEA WHAT YOU LOSERS ARE TALKING ABOUT. IT MUST BE TIME FOR YOUR MEDS!

But I had a feeling in my gut that she was lying.

"It doesn't belong to you, so give it back," I demanded.

"Well, maybe I have it. Or maybe I don't! You'll never—"

MacKenzie stopped midsentence, distracted by something behind us. Her frown quickly melted into a dazzling—but very fake—smile.

I turned around just as Principal Winston came striding into the office. "Good afternoon, girls!" he said.

"Oh, my! Look at the time. Gotta run! See you in geometry, Nikki." MacKenzie grabbed her purse and nervously bolted for the door.

I traded glances with Chloe and Zoey. They quickly stepped in front of her, blocking her path so she couldn't leave.

MacKenzie shot them both a dirty look, but it was too late.

I took a deep breath. "Hi, Principal Winston. I was wondering if you could help us with a small problem?"

He stopped and adjusted his glasses. "Sure! Now, what seems to be the trouble?"

MacKenzie fluttered her eyelashes innocently and tried to take control of the situation. "Actually, Principal Winston, the problem is that Nikki here seems to think I have a book that belongs to her."

"I don't think it. I KNOW it!" I snapped.

MacKenzie sniffed and pretended to be on the verge of tears. "I was just telling her that I don't have her stupid diary. But she doesn't believe me. I have no idea why she would say such a mean thing about me after I've been so nice to her and gave her all that free fashion advice. And just look at her, Principal Winston. She really needs it. Our mascot, Larry the Lizard, has a better wardrobe than she does—"

"Then how did you even know my diary was missing? Or that it has a pocket on the cover?" I demanded.

Everyone in the room, including Principal Winston, just stared at her, waiting for her answer.

MacKenzie bit her lip and started to squirm.

"Well, actually . . . um, the whole school knows. Chloe and Zoey announced it during gym. And you write in it every single day. That's how I know it has a pocket on the cover. But I swear! I don't have it!"

"These types of allegations will not be taken lightly," Principal Winston said sternly, and folded his arms. "I hope you girls can work this out, because if I get involved . . ."

MacKenzie's face flushed, and she glanced at her purse.

"Okay, Nikki! If you don't believe me, go ahead! Check my purse!" Then she sniffed and blinked back more phony tears for dramatic effect.

She removed four tubes of lip gloss, Tic Tacs, and a brush from her purse and placed them on the counter.

Then she closed her eyes and held out her purse like she was surrendering her new puppy to an unusually cruel dog catcher.

MacKenzie's purse was EMPTY!

All I could do was stare in complete shock.

What had that girl done with my DIARY?!

"Thank you, Miss Hollister!" Principal Winston said approvingly.

"I'm VERY impressed with your integrity."

But I was totally baffled! How had she tricked me like that?

"WELL . . . ?!" Winston glared at me and began drumming his fingers impatiently.

"Um, I guess sh-she doesn't have my d-diary after all," I muttered.

I felt so embarrassed. I wanted to grab the office wastebasket and wear it to cover up the word "IDIOT" that had just been stamped on my forehead.

Chloe, Zoey, and I traded nervous glances.

"Well, Miss Maxwell, I think you owe Miss Hollister an apology," Winston said as MacKenzie smiled like a little angel who had just earned her wings.

I was so angry I wanted to . . . SPIT!

It took every ounce of my willpower not to slap that SMUG little SMIRK right off her face!!

I stared down at my feet and tried to swallow the large lump in my throat.

"Um, I—I'm sorry!" I mumbled.

"Huh? What did she say? I couldn't hear her!" MacKenzie whined like a spoiled brat.

"I said, 'I'm SORRY'!"

"Now, Miss Maxwell, I hope you'll think twice before you wrongly accuse someone like this again. Do you understand, young lady?"

I hung my head. "Yes, sir. . ."

Winston glanced at his watch. "Well, girls, I have a conference call in exactly two minutes. I'm glad we were able to resolve this issue to everyone's satisfaction."

Then he strode into his office and closed the door.

As Chloe and Zoey walked me back to my locker, my head was spinning. "I feel SO stupid! I'm sorry I dragged you guys into this," I muttered.

"Hey, don't worry about it," Zoey said. "We thought MacKenzie had your diary too."

"You have to admit, she WAS acting pretty suspicious," Chloe agreed. "But don't worry, Nikki. I'm sure your diary will turn up when we least expect it."

In spite of everything that had just happened, I still had this nagging feeling in my gut that MacKenzie was not as innocent as she was pretending to be.

And now if my diary ends up plastered all over the bathroom stalls, Principal Winston will NOT even consider her a suspect.

MacKenzie is going to get away with ruining my life, and there is nothing I can do to stop her.

I really hate to admit it, but she totally set me up. AGAIN!! ☹!!

NOTE TO SELF

It's helpful to have a good memory when keeping a diary so later you can write about all the stuff that happened to you.

OMG! I almost DIED when I saw Brandon in the cereal aisle. We stared at each other for what felt like forever. And when we both grabbed the same box of Fruity Pebbles, he actually smiled at me. I came home in a complete DAZE. And now that I remember what happened, I realize . . .

. . . I ACCIDENTALLY LEFT BRIANNA AT THE GROCERY STORE!! AAAHHH!!!!

HOW TO DORK YOUR DIARY TIP #12

DON'T FORGET TO REMEMBER.

What did you have for breakfast this morning?

What was the cutest outfit you saw, and who was wearing it?

_____
_____
_____
_____
_____
_____
_____
_____
_____

What was the last song you
listened to?

_____

_____

_____

_____

_____

_____

_____

Did you talk to anybody on the
phone? What did you talk about?

_____

_____

_____

_____

_____

_____

What was the funniest thing you
heard today, and who said it?

_____

_____

_____

_____

_____

_____

What was the smartest thing you
said all day?

_____

_____

_____

_____

_____

Did you dream last night? If so,
what did you dream about?

_____

_____

_____

LIBRARY, 2:35 p.m.

I'm SO upset at MacKenzie, I can barely focus on shelving library books.

I just KNOW she has my diary.

But after that SUPERembarrassing fiasco with Principal Winston, it was quite obvious that MacKenzie wasn't stupid enough to hide my diary in her purse and risk getting caught with it.

But if MacKenzie doesn't have it,

WHO DOES ☹?!!

I'm SO thoroughly confused! I feel like I am drowning in a tidal wave of hopelessness.

Just the thought of my diary being passed around and read by everyone like the latest edition of the school newspaper makes me feel sick to my stomach.

Blinking back tears, I sighed and stared out of the library window. Since our football team has a game tomorrow, they were on the field practicing.

I wondered how many of them

WHO WANTS TO READ NIKKI MAXWELL'S DIARY?! GET YOUR FREE COPY RIGHT HERE!

would read my diary and then go out of their way to make my life miserable. Lunchtime is going to be unbearable!

I was pretty sure Brady, our star quarterback, would be the ringleader. Not only has he been crushing on MacKenzie lately, but she got busted in biology texting him and—

That's when it hit me like a ton of bricks!

"OMG! OMG! CHLOE! ZOEY! I THINK I KNOW WHO HAS MY DIARY . . .!!!"

IN THE HALL OUTSIDE THE BOYS' LOCKER ROOM, 2:45 p.m.

NO WAY! I COULDN'T possibly do this!

WHY?! Because someone could end up DEAD, that's why.

Namely . . . ME ☹!!

Chloe and Zoey came up with their CRAZIEST scheme yet. And I knew for sure that:

1. Their plan would NEVER work.

2. We were going to get caught.

3. We were going to get suspended from school.

Then my parents are going to

KILL ME ☹!!

And if I'm DEAD, I'll probably NEVER, EVER find my diary!

The three of us had bathroom passes, so we were SUPPOSED to be in the girls' bathroom.

But NOOOOOO!!!

We were slinking around outside the boys' locker room.

Mainly because Chloe, Zoey, and I had all come to the unanimous conclusion that my diary was in there.

It HAD to be!

We think MacKenzie gave it to Brady and they were texting each other about it.

Since the football players are now on the field practicing, Brady's duffel bag was somewhere in the boys' locker room.

"All we have to do is simply walk inside, find the locker with Brady's duffel bag, and grab your diary!" Zoey whispered so loudly, her voice seemed to be echoing through the halls and into every classroom on this side of the building.

"Are you KA-RAY-ZEE?!!" I hissed back at her. "What if we get caught?!"

"Don't worry!" Chloe assured me. "Just ask yourself what the heroine of your favorite novel would do in this situation."

"Yeah, right!" I muttered. "So where in the world am I supposed to find a prom dress and a pack of shirtless werewolf boys on a Friday afternoon? I'm just

saying!"

Chloe rolled her eyes at me.

I really appreciated that Chloe and Zoey were trying to help me find my diary and all. But I have to admit, some days I seriously worry about those two.

"No one has gone in or come out in the last few minutes," Chloe whispered. "I don't think anyone's in there!"

"Listen, guys," I began, "I think we should just go back to the library before we—"

"OKAY! Let's make a run for it!!" Zoey said excitedly.

Before I could say, "What the . . . !!" Chloe and Zoey rushed the boys' locker room door and poked their heads inside.

"OMG! CHLOEEEE!! ZOEEEEY!! NOO!" I scream-whispered at the top of my lungs.

But it was too late. I didn't

have any choice but to go after them.

OMG!

I could NOT BELIEVE I was actually in the boys' locker room!! It's a large, square room with lockers along three walls.

ME, Zoey, AND Chloe PEEKING INSIDE THE BOYS' LOCKER ROOM!!

It's a lot bigger than the girls' locker room and has an area with a line of those boy-toilet thingies.

Chloe, Zoey, and I quickly began searching inside each locker, one after another.

"Hurry!" Zoey yelled over her shoulder. "It's posted by the door that there's a swim team meeting in here in ten minutes, so we don't have much time!"

I fought the overwhelming urge to panic and run out of there screaming.

We had just about made our way around the entire room, with no luck. Then, as I was opening the second-to-last locker, I spotted Brady's name on a duffel bag.

"That good-for-nothing, meathead crook," I muttered, sorting through the stuff in his bag.

I felt a small book underneath a Spider-Man comic.

I couldn't contain my excitement! "Chloe! Zoey! I found it!" I screamed.

They came rushing over and crowded around me.

"You have to be a real slimeball to steal a girl's . . . Cupcakes for Every Occasion, cookbook?!" I sputtered. I held the book in front of me in shock and disappointment.

On the cover were cupcakes decorated like puppies and kittens. I felt their licorice smiles mocking me.

But there was no time for me to grieve over the fact that my diary was still out there somewhere.

I heard a man's booming voice and heavy footsteps coming toward the locker room door. Did I mention that it's the ONLY locker room door?

My heart skipped a beat. Chloe and Zoey froze.

They looked at me, and then in the direction of the approaching man, with sheer terror in their eyes. There was no way we were going to make it out of there alive.

We stared in horror as a hairy hand pushed the door open halfway . . . and then froze!

". . . What do you mean we have only two buses for the game tomorrow? I specifically ordered THREE buses! How are we supposed to play with only part of our team?! I might as well just cancel! No, I'm NOT canceling. I said . . . What? Can I hold? You have another call? No! I can't hold! I need my buses!! . . ."

The guy was having a telephone conversation right there in the doorway. And lucky for us, a VERY long one.

That's when I noticed the huge cart of dirty football uniforms and equipment about ten feet away.

"Chloe! Zoey!" I whispered, and pointed.

The girls immediately understood my plan. Within seconds the three of us were at that cart.

We grabbed football jerseys, pants, helmets, and shoes, and we dressed faster than we ever had in our entire lives. And just in time!

Coach "Rowdy" Rowling's nostrils flared when he saw us standing there in our football uniforms twiddling our thumbs.

"What the Sam Hill is this?" he shouted. "Why do I have three players in here hangin' around like they're waiting for the city bus? What's your excuse, Clayton?"

He pointed at Zoey, who was wearing a jersey that said "Clayton" on the back. She shook so badly her helmet rattled.

"Answer me! What's wrong, Clayton? Cat got your tongue?"

"M-men are not prisoners of fate, but only prisoners of their own minds," she stuttered. "Franklin D. Roosevelt."

Coach Rowling furrowed his brow and stared at Zoey like she had just answered him in Swedish.

"That don't even make sense! You think you're funny? How 'bout y'all doin' twenty laps around the track and then hittin' the showers?

Now, THAT'S funny!"

Someone standing outside the locker room door cleared his throat rather loudly. "Excuse me, Coach . . ."

Me, Chloe, Zoey, and Coach Rowling turned to see who it was.

Brandon stood in the doorway with his camera around his neck.

OMG! I almost FAINTED right there on the spot!

"I'm here to take your photo for the Coach of the Year article. Did I catch you at a bad time?"

Coach Rowling stood up straight and regained his composure. "Not at all, son. I was just goin' over the strategy for our big game tomorrow," he lied. "These boys will tell you I run a tight ship, which is why we never lose. Nothin' gets past me. No, sir!" Coach Rowling chuckled and gave me a playful punch on my shoulder.

"OW!" I whimpered before

thinking. "I mean, 'OWW!'" I said in my deepest boyish voice.

Brandon stared at me, then Chloe, and then Zoey for what seemed like forever.

Shaking his head, he blinked in disbelief.

WE WERE SO BUSTED!

"Hey, let's head outside. You can take some pictures of me in action." Coach Rowling did one of those corny poses like he was running the ball downfield.

"Actually . . . would you mind if I steal these guys from practice?" Brandon asked, pointing to Chloe, Zoey, and me. "I, um, want to interview them for the article so readers will know just how, um . . . awesome you are as a coach."

"He's only the most awesomest coach EVER!"

I croaked in my horrible boy voice.

"He's the man!" grunted Zoey.

"Yeah, bro," added Chloe. "And he lets us do cool guy stuff, like burp. And hit things. And play in the ball pit at Queasy Cheesy and—"

I gave her a hard kick to zip it. Clearly, the only boy Chloe knows is her little brother, Joey.

"Right!" Brandon laughed nervously. "So . . . anyway, Coach, is that cool with you? Once I interview Team Rowling, I can take your photo."

"Team Rowling? I like the sound of that. Take as much time as you need. When you're ready, I'll be out on the field."

Coach Rowling winked and then headed out the door.

We stood in silence until it shut behind him.

"Nikki, Chloe, Zoey! WHAT are you doing dressed like football players in the BOYS' locker room?!" Brandon asked.

"Actually, I can explain." I took off my helmet. "We were looking for my diary. We thought MacKenzie might have given it to Brady. So we decided to check his duffel bag." I hung my head in shame. "But I was wrong. He didn't have it."

"Well, you guys better get out of here! Before Coach remembers those laps and comes looking for you."

"Thanks for saving our skins," Zoey said.

"No problem. I hope you find your diary, Nikki."

Brandon gave me a sincere smile that normally would've made me melt like a Popsicle.

But, given the fact that my life was over, I only mustered a half smile. "Thank you, Brandon. We really appreciate you helping us out of this mess!" I said.

But in my heart I felt all hope was lost.

I didn't want to put my friends or MYSELF through any more drama.

NOTE TO MY FUTURE SELF:
Dear Future Self,

If you're reading this, I've

probably been publicly humiliated and banished by MacKenzie to an unknown island in the Pacific.

Even though I am now a freaky hermit person, please let Brianna know she's still not allowed to go into my room. I hope things worked out for you and Brandon.

Love, Nikki Maxwell

P.S. Please burn this diary so no one else can read it.

NOTE TO SELF

One of the best parts about a diary is that you can look back at all the silly things you said years, months, weeks, days, and even hours ago. It's common to read entries from the past.

But if you think about it, a diary is almost like a time machine to both your past AND your future!

HOW?

You can write an entry to your future self, then come back and read it later!

Weird, huh?

But VERY COOL!

HOW TO DORK YOUR DIARY TIP #13

BE PEN PALS WITH YOUR FUTURE SELF!

What would you say to the eighteen-year-old version of yourself? Write a letter to your eighteen-year-old self.

Dear Eighteen-Year-Old Me,

_____

_____

_____

_____

_____

_____

Writing in your diary should be a pleasant experience. Whenever possible, try to write in a quiet place where you won't be disturbed or distracted.

HOW TO DORK YOUR DIARY TIP #14

FIND A COMFY SPOT AND CHILLAX AS YOU WRITE.

Where would you choose for your secret diary-writing hideout?

_____

_____

_____

_____

_____

_____

_____

_____

_____

_____

Sincerely,

_____ -Year-Old Me

ME, IN MY SECRET
DIARY-WRITING
HIDEOUT!

Draw a picture of yourself writing in your diary in your secret hideout.

AT HOME, 4:00 p.m.

WHY, WHY, WHY is my life SO horrendously CRUDDY ☹?!

I think my diary is LOST FOREVER.

Especially since MacKenzie is looking for it too.

I would have sworn she had it in her purse in the office, but I guess I was wrong.

I think she was only pretending to have my diary so that I'd give up and stop looking for it. Having me totally out of the picture would've greatly improved her chances of actually finding it.

I know it's kind of complicated. But MacKenzie makes EVERYTHING complicated.

I am so NOT looking forward to having the entire school reading all of my personal business.

But I guess I'll survive it.

Just like I've managed to survive all the other major disasters in my pathetic little life.

Thank goodness my BFFs, Chloe and Zoey, have got my back.

I still can't believe they were willing to risk going into the boys' locker room like that, just to help me find my diary.

They're the best friends EVER!

Right now I'm a bundle of raw nerves and conflicting emotions.

I FEEL HAPPY, ANGRY, RELIEVED, AND SUPER-INSECURE ALL AT THE SAME TIME.

WHY?

I was in the middle of throwing a massive pity party for myself when Brianna came rushing in from school, screaming at the top of her lungs.

"Nikki! Nikki! I have very happy news! You'll never guess what happened in school today!"

I was drinking a bottle of water, because throwing a pity party is exhausting work and can make you very hot and thirsty.

I was so shocked, I didn't

ME, TAKING A SHORT BREAK
FROM MY PITY PARTY TO
DRINK A BOTTLED WATER

"BRIANNA! YOU TOOK MY DIARY
TO SCHOOL FOR SHOW-AND-
TELL??!!" I screamed.

know whether to YELL at her
for taking it or THANK her for
returning it. But since I no longer
had to worry about MacKenzie
plastering pages of my diary

around the school, it was actually
a no-brainer.

I gave my bratty little sister a
humongous bear hug!

Then I made Brianna pinkie-
promise to NEVER, EVER touch
my stuff again without asking
for permission first. Our little
ceremony was such a bonding
experience for us as sisters, I
almost shed a tear. . .

WITH MY PINKIE,
I PROMISE AND PLEDGE
TO NEVER TAKE OR BORROW.

'CAUSE NIKKI WILL BE
SO MAD AT ME,
SHE'LL KNOCK ME INTO
TOMORROW!

Of course, being the pathological liar that she is, Brianna totally denied taking my diary.

"Miss Penelope stole your stupid diary, not ME! I told her not to do it, but she didn't even listen to me!"

That was Brianna's story, and she was sticking to it.

Although, now that I think about it, Miss Penelope and MacKenzie have a lot in common:

1. They are both SUPERannoying.

2. They both have a HUGE MOUTH.

3. They both wear WAY too much lip gloss.

4. They both enjoy TORTURING me.

5. They both have NO BRAIN whatsoever.

OMG! They're probably identical twins who were separated at birth!!

But I have to admit, I'm not perfect either.

Seriously, folks . . .

I'M SUCH A DORK ☺!!

NOTE TO SELF
A diary is a great place to get supercreative. Try writing a poem or the lyrics to an original song. Poetry can rhyme or be free verse (which means it doesn't rhyme). Although this might seem like a difficult or boring task, it's actually EASY and FUN! Think about your favorite rapper or rap song. Rap is just another form of poetry!

HOW TO DORK YOUR DIARY TIP #15

WRITING POETRY IS A

SNAP WHEN YOU THINK OF IT AS RAP.

First you're going to need a stage name. You can add "MC" or "LIL" to your own name or make up something silly. Write your rap, poem, or song on the next page. Hey! You're a poet and dont know it.

_____
title of your poem

_____
_____
_____
_____
_____
_____
_____
_____
_____
_____
_____
_____
_____
_____
_____
_____
_____
_____
_____
_____
_____
_____
_____

by _____
your stage name

NOTE TO SELF

Your diary belongs to YOU and no one else (no matter what your bratty little sister might think). So you can write about your day, your crush, your favorite things, a party you want to throw, or absolutely anything else you want to write about, anytime you want!

HOW TO DORK YOUR DIARY TIP #16

WRITE ABOUT ANYTHING, EVERYTHING, OR NOTHING— IT'S YOUR DIARY!

EEEEE! Flip the corners of the pages to see Nikki's Snoopy "happy dance"! →

Rachel Renée Russell is an attorney who prefers writing tween books to legal briefs. (Mainly because books are a lot more fun and pajamas and bunny slippers aren't allowed in court.)

She has raised two daughters and lived to tell about it. Her hobbies include growing purple flowers and doing totally useless crafts (like, for example, making a microwave oven out of Popsicle sticks, glue, and glitter). Rachel lives in northern Virginia with a spoiled pet Yorkie who terrorizes her daily by climbing on top of a computer cabinet and pelting her with stuffed animals while she writes. And, yes, Rachel considers herself a total Dork.